MW01618652

This special edition is limited to
1,000 signed copies.

destinations UNKNOWN

destinations UNKNOWN

GARY A. BRAUNBECK

CEMETERY DANCE PUBLICATIONS

Baltimore

❖ 2006 ❖

Signed Hardcover Edition ISBN 1-58767-085-2
Destinations Unknown

This book is a work of fiction. Names, characters, places, and incidents are either a product of the author's imagination or are used fictitiously. Any resemblance to actual events or locales or persons, living or dead, is entirely coincidental.

Manufactured in the United States of America.

FIRST EDITION

Cemetery Dance Publications
132-B Industry Lane
Unit 7
Forest Hill, MD 21050
Email: info@cemeterydance.com

www.cemeterydance.com

To everyone who has suffered through the cruel and unusual punishment of having me for a passenger during a road trip.

I'm really sorry.

Really *sorry.*

table of CONTENTS

"Well it's a winding highway that never seems to end…"
— Rory Gallagher, "Lonesome Highway"

"…Abe said, 'Where you want this killin' done?'
God said, 'Out on Highway 61…'"
— Bob Dylan, "Highway 61 Revisited"

the ballad of ROAD MAMA and DADDY BLISS

It could have been a scene from any drive-in B-feature from the 1950s or early '60s featuring juvenile delinquents as Everyman and drag racing as heavy-handed social metaphor:

FADE IN: A seemingly endless stretch of smooth two-lane blacktop emptying into shadows. Crowds of people line both sides of the road, the men looking tough while clutching at their bottles of beer, the women looking anxious while clutching at the filtered tips of their cigarettes, and the kids—especially the really young ones—looking like they aren't sure *how* they should be feeling while they clutch at the hands or coats of the tough beer drinkers and anxious cigarette smokers.

There are dozens of cars parked at haphazard angles off to the side, their headlights illuminating two vehicles that crouch rumbling in the center of the strip, rabid animals straining at the leash. A YOUNG GIRL, early twenties (if that), dressed in a skirt and tight short-sleeved sweater, blonde hair pulled back into a ponytail, a scarf tied around her neck, stands a few dozen feet from the front of the cars, raising her arms above her head with a slow dramatic relish, a bright red kerchief clutched in each of her hands…

I was trying very hard to imagine all of this as being a scene from a movie that I was watching, half-expecting one of the SUPPORTING CHARACTERS to scream something profound like, "Burn rubber, Daddy-O!" so I could smile at all the clichés being firmly in place. If I could achieve some kind of half-assed Zen state, if I could convince myself that I wasn't really a part of all this, if I could delude myself into believing that I was just viewing it from a safe distance, then I might be able to survive the next two minutes with mind and body in one piece—providing I could force myself to overlook the physical appearance of most of the spectators, or the *thing* that was driving the car I was about to race against. I could try focusing on the blonde girl who was about to signal the start of the race, but that would mean looking at her arms, both of which were easily about six inches longer than a normal arm is supposed to be, her elbows having been replaced by the type of steel hinges used to fasten car hoods to their vehicles; what sinew, veins, and muscle remained to connect her forearms to her biceps wound through and around the hinges like vines, all of it kept functional with a combination of machine grease and petroleum jelly.

And she was one of the more *normal*-looking spectators here tonight.

"On your marks," she shouted, her arms now raised to their full height, the crowd silent, wide-eyed, leaning forward.

The other vehicle gunned its engine, its driver letting fly with a phlegm-clogged laugh from a throat equal parts metal and meat.

Tightening my grip on the steering wheel, I wondered if I squeezed hard enough, would my knuckles just rip through my skin. Maybe they'd postpone the race if I were injured.

One quick look at my opponent answered that question in short order.

The blonde girl was smiling a smile that might have been radiant in any other place, under any other circumstances. "*Get set…*"

Her grip tightened on the kerchiefs in her hands. In a moment, she'd swing down those impossible arms in a swift, decisive arc, and off we'd go.

I closed my eyes and took a deep breath, wondering how long I'd be missing and dead before anyone took serious notice of my absence. It was quite the revelation, it was, to realize that out of all my friends…I didn't really have any.

Have to move that to the top of your "To Do" list right away, I thought. *Numero uno: make some friends…and try to keep them this time. Abso-freakin-lutely.*

Oh, yeah—I was *so* boned.

The other vehicle gunned its engine once more, snapping me out of my maudlin reverie with an earsplitting reminder that very likely I would be dead one-hundred-and-thirty seconds from now.

The blonde-haired girl stood frozen, ready to snap down her arms.

The spectators leaned farther forward, still and silent.

I took a deep breath and without consciously trying achieved the elusive *faux*-Zen state I'd been hoping for, only I wasn't watching *this* scene from a distance, no; I was watching the me of roughly forty hours ago, the me who'd been safe and sound in the world he knew well enough to take for granted, the me who was about to learn that…

1

"…sometimes the bodies leak."

I looked over at the man driving the meat wagon in which I was currently a court-required passenger and said, ever the fellow armed with a witty retort: "*Huh?*"

The driver—a fifty-something guy named Fred Dobbs (I'm not kidding; just like the character Bogart played in *The Treasure of the Sierra Madre,* swear to God), a man built like a walk-in freezer who was also a twenty-two-year veteran driver for the County Coroner's Office—nodded his head and sighed as if empathizing, though he was trying hard to conceal a grin. "Yeah, whenever we get a call like this one—y'know, when the folks have been dead a day or two—sometimes you're gonna find that the bodies have been laying in the bed or on the floor, and if the weather's all hot and humid like it's been and they ain't got airconditioning, the internal gasses build up a *whole* lot faster and then things start to strain and tear and rupture and the bodies, well…sometimes they leak when you move 'em." He cleared his throat, and when he spoke again his tone was much lighter, as if telling a joke: "I once had so much trouble trying to get this one old gal out of her bed—her bedsores were so bad that I thought her skin was gonna peel off and dump her guts right on my shoes—I finally just had to wrap her up in the sheets she'd died in before transferring her to the bag. If it's bad, then we let the wizards in the doc's office do the peeling. Our job is to just get in there and remove the bodies."

"Which sometimes leak."

Another nod: the teacher pleased that the student wasn't as dim as he'd feared. "I'm not trying to make you sick or nothing, understand, but I figured maybe you ought to prepare yourself for the possibility." He shrugged, honked the horn for reasons I'd never know at someone or something I couldn't see, then removed one of his hands from the steering wheel and flexed his fingers, the bones crackling like dry twigs on a campfire.

I reached out to turn down the radio; the news had been talking about a massive (what they called "…spectacular") eight-car accident in Columbus on the I-71 loop last night that so far had left five people dead. The radio station had someone broadcasting live from the scene which *still* hadn't been cleared. It appeared the accident had been caused when someone driving a Hummer cut across all four lanes without signaling and slammed into a Ford Gargantuan or some other four-wheeled yuppie tank that in turn hit a semi…and I didn't want to hear about it. There's only so much death and destruction I can take when the sun is shining and there's still the possibility of having a nice day.

"'Course, now," said Dobbs, "if the bodies're on a rug or carpeting, that makes it a bit easier in some ways. If they're leaking all over a rug, we just roll 'em up in it and save the county the cost of a bag."

"And if they've leaked onto the carpeting?" Pause for a moment and consider: how many people get to start their workday with conversations like this? Was I the luckiest guy on the planet, or what?

"Then we haul out the carpet cutters and…" He mimed scissoring around a body. "But then you've got the added problem of some extra weight if they've *really* been leaking, and *especially* if it's shag carpeting."

I shook my head. "*Damn* the shag carpeting!"

"Oh, you got *that* right. Me, I think that shit makes any room look like something that belongs in a porno movie—not that I've seen all *that* many pornos, you understand, it's just there's something kinda…I dunno…sleazy and tacky about it."

Gas-ruptured bodies and home decorating tips. With lunch still hours away. My life was an embarrassment of blessings.

I looked in the back of the wagon where a crate hand-labeled **Retrieval Gear** sat with its unlocked lid bouncing up and down every time we drove over a pothole. Symbolic thoughts of Pandora's Box notwithstanding, the sight gave me the creeps, knowing as I did what was inside.

"Do you think we'll have to use any of the science fiction paraphernalia?"

Dobbs seriously considered this; I knew he was considering it seriously because the right side of his face knotted up as if he were having a stroke. "Hard to say. I kinda like putting on them HazMat suits myself. Scares the hell out of people and they keep outta your way. I used to feel silly wearing that stuff until the doc explained to me that dead, leaking bodies produce their own kind of toxic waste." He looked at me and, for the first time that morning, smiled outright; there was a lot of genuine kindness it. "Don't you worry none. If it's bad, I'll walk you through it. I know this ain't exactly what you had in mind, and I may act like a royal horse's ass most of the time—at least according to anyone who's known me for more than twenty minutes—but I got sympathy."

"You've had assistants like me before?"

He barked a loud laugh. “Hell, buddy, how do you think *I* got started on this job?”

“You’re kidding?”

“If I was kidding, don’t you think I’d try to come up with something funnier than that?”

“Good point.”

He gave a short, sharp nod. “They got me same way as you. Had one too many before hitting the road one night and got stopped by Johnny Law. Since I’d drove an ambulance in Vietnam, judge figured that me and the meat wagon was a perfect community-service match.” He shrugged. “When my CS period was done, they offered me a permanent job.” He looked at me. “I actually kinda *like* it. Dead folks’re quiet, and I treat them with respect, even when I gotta roll ‘em up in sheets or rugs.”

“Or shag carpeting.”

He almost grinned. “I don’t make no jokes when I’m taking care of them. The doc likes that, likes my attitude, which is why I can get away with some of the shit that I pull, and whenever the city does its budget-cut dance, like they done here last quarter, I don’t have to worry about being left out of work.”

“That explains why I wasn’t given a choice in the matter.” My lawyer had told me that the courts try to match your own individual abilities to a county department where those abilities could best be used, which is why I’d expected to find myself cleaning offices—I’m a crew manager with a local janitorial company—but Judge Walter Banks was in a bad mood, evidently being pressured to assign more defendants to CS duty (*damn* the budget cuts!), and said he’d had his fill of “…people who think they’ve got the constitution of an ox so they don’t think twice about getting behind the wheel while under the influence…" and slapped me with both a five hundred dollar fine and one hundred hours of community service. My lawyer argued that, by law, I was to be given a choice of assignments; Judge Banks pointed out that the matter of being offered a choice was up to the discretion of the bench, and his particular bench felt that I damned well ought to be exposed to the dead in order to remind me of what *could have* happened had I hit a pedestrian or another car.

So I was assigned to the budget-strapped County Coroner's Office. As Fred Dobbs' assistant. In the passenger seat of the meat wagon. Talk about your pot of gold at the end of the rainbow.

"By the way," I said, "I wasn't drunk."

"Of course you weren't. And every man on Death Row is innocent."

"I'm not trying to say I didn't *deserve* my fine and the rest of it, I just want it made clear that I wasn't drunk."

"But you *were* half-snowed on Demerol."

"I'd gotten slammed with a migraine, I went to the ER, they gave me a shot—"

"—and probably told you not to drive yourself home, isn't that right?"

I shrugged. "I thought I could make it home before the stuff really kicked in."

"Appears you were mistaken."

I shrugged. "Hell, I was probably more dangerous driving *to* the hospital than I was driving home afterward."

"Hate to be the one to break the news to you, but 'under the influence' don't just refer to drinking, you know."

"I do now."

Dobbs sighed, rubbing one of his eyes. "You're not gonna grouse like this for the next three weeks, are you? Unless it's the sound of my own voice—which I find soothing and not without a certain musical quality—I kinda prefer to keep the conversation upbeat."

"I didn't think I was complaining."

"Maybe not, but you were in the neighborhood. Speaking of—double-check the address for me, would you?"

I picked up the clipboard and read the address to him.

"You sure that's right?"

I offered the board to him; he stopped at a red light, took the board, and read it for himself. "Huh. That's odd."

"What?"

"When Doc said East Main, I just kinda assumed it was the Taft Hotel. A lot of old folks and welfare cases wind up croaking there."

I was familiar with the Taft; hell, anyone who's lived here for more than a year knows about it. Once the most popular and expensive hotel in the city (named after William Howard Taft, who'd frequently stayed there), the last fifty years have seen it slide not-so-slowly into disrepair and decay, becoming nothing more than a glorified flop-house where those who've reached the end of their rope can crawl into poverty's shadow and just give up. I'd assumed, as well, that the Taft was our destination, but it turned out we were headed for The Maples, an apartment building located two miles farther down East Main Street. The Maples' residents were exclusively those elderly who still had their wits and retirement funds very much about them, and who were capable of living unsupervised. The Maples had good security, two doctors who lived on-site, an exercise room, a small chapel for Sunday services (some residents could not drive to church, so church came to them), and touted itself as the place to go for "…those seniors who can still do it on their own." My grandmother had lived there until her death three years ago. Though I hadn't set foot in its lobby since then, I had no reason to think that The Maples had suffered a fate similar to that of the Taft.

"Well," said Dobbs, tossing down the clipboard as the light turned green, "I think we can rule out having to wear the spacesuits today."

"Another thrill my life will have to do without."

"I can feel your heartbreak all the way over here."

I picked up the clipboard and looked at the sheet again. Under **Caller's Name**, the space was blank.

"Aren't they supposed to take the name of whoever calls it in?" I asked.

"*Supposed* to. The city's *supposed* to have fixed all the potholes in the road, I'm *supposed* to weigh thirty-five pounds less than I do, and you're *supposed* to be doing something else besides helping me. For that matter, this whole to-do was *supposed* to be handled by the book, but there ain't been nothing about this has gone like it's *supposed* to."

"Meaning…?"

"Meaning that the doc was *ordered* by the mayor to examine the body hisownself. Doc doesn't do that unless it's a murder scene. Some old lady croaks in her apartment or a hotel room or at a nursing home, he sends one of his flunkies to look over the body and make the call to whatever funeral home is gonna be handling it." He shook his head. "Not this time, no sir—*this* time the doc is ordered to do it personally. Mayor called him at home around five this morning, made the man get out of bed and go to it pronto. Doc was awfully tight-lipped about everything when he called me about the paperwork. Can't say I'm too happy about being kept out of the loop."

I remembered the call; it had come into the office just as I arrived for work. Dobbs had seemed confused as he looked at the forms left on his desk by the coroner—his end of the conversation consisted of, "Yes sir", and "But why—?", and "We'll get on it right now." It seemed like an awfully short exchange, considering what we were being sent out to do.

"So," I said, "you're supposed to be given more information than this?"

Dobbs nodded. "Yeah, but like I said, *supposed to* don't always cut it. My guess is that one of the neighbors found her, told the building manager, and the manager called the police, cha-cha-cha—though why in hell the *mayor* got involved in this is beyond me. We can always ask whatever poor doofus the department left on the scene."

"There's gonna be a cop there?"

He nodded. "There's *always* a cop there until we show up. Once foul play has been ruled out—and that's already been done—what you're left with is a body that's just laying there stinking up the place and making everyone else nervous as hell. The law doesn't require that an officer remain with the body until it's picked up, but it ain't exactly like Cedar Hill is Miami. They can spare an officer to corpse-sit for an hour or so."

"I'll bet that puts them in a cheery frame of mind."

"Well, we're gonna be finding out here in a minute or three."

He drove the wagon into the Maples' underground parking garage, expertly backing up so that the rear doors faced the freight elevator. We got out, unloaded and unfolded the collapsible gurney, grabbed the clipboard, Latex gloves for each of us, some scissors in case there was carpet work to be done, a couple of filter masks, and then, finally, the body bag.

Dobbs pressed the button, stood waiting for a moment, then shook his head and said, "Shit, I forgot, come on." He started walking toward one of the parking garage doors that led into the lobby. "We have to get the elevator key from whoever's manning the front desk."

A set of glass doors opened into a warmly-lit hallway with gold carpeting. On the walls hung bulletin boards with announcements and fliers tacked on them—Bingo Night, a pot-luck dinner at a local church, a lecture on living wills to be given at the library next week—as well as tastefully-framed prints showing bowls of fruit, glamorous cityscapes, and myriad pastoral scenes. The furniture was clean and over-stuffed, the sofa pillows fluffy, the doilies and afghans perfectly folded and arranged, the whole setting designed to make you feel Right At Home. Smells of soup, cornbread, and meatloaf wafted from the cafeteria (**The Maples' Dining Room**, as it was called by the sign), and the murmuring of the voices coming from the dining area suggested that it was filled with people who'd known each other for decades and could easily fall into the kind of familiar, friendly conversation that, between lifelong friends, becomes a kind of art unto itself.

Despite my increasing anxiety over what Fred and I were about to do, I slowed down, chancing a glance into the dining room, then stopped in my tracks entirely when I saw how everyone was dressed; the women wore either dresses or attractive suit outfits, while all the men were in slacks, jackets, and ties. I looked around, trying to see if there were anything posted about a dress code, and then just as quickly realized there wouldn't be. This dining room was filled with people who remembered what it was like to treat mealtime as an event, every day. You dressed for meals not only out of respect for yourself, but for those with whom you would share the meal. Looking at the diners at that moment, I found myself wondering when, how, and why we'd come to view what was meant to be a sociable event of the day as just another excuse to grab some chow. Me, I frequently ate alone while wearing only my underwear, and the last time I'd had a dinner date, I'd worn khakis and a polo shirt, while my date arrived resplendent in her jeans, sandals, and OSU sweatshirt. Maybe we think it's too old-fashioned or outright corny to dress like this for meals every day, but I'd've bet a week's salary that every person in there had spent a lot of time deciding what to wear, then just as much time getting ready, and were probably enjoying their meal more than we of the jeans-and-T-shirted pizza nights could or would ever understand.

Somebody has to come up with these commonplace profundities. Might as well be me.

I smiled at an old woman who looked up and saw me looming in the doorway, then double-timed it to catch up with Dobbs, who was speaking to the receptionist at the front desk.

"…moved in about seven months ago," the woman was saying, "and in all that time I don't remember her ever having a single visitor."

Dobbs gave his head a slow, sad shake. "That's terrible," he said, sounding like he meant it.

"One of the things we try to do here at The Maples is make sure that none of our residents feel isolated—it's a terrible thing to be getting on in years and feel alone and lonely. We encourage everyone to interact with their neighbors—you know, sort of keep an eye on each other's well-being so that no one feels ignored or forgotten...but Miss Driscoll never really allowed herself to become part of The Maples' community. Oh, she'd be pleasant enough at meals and come to the weekly residents' meetings, but aside from those times, she rarely left her room."

Fred put on his stroke-face again, considering this. "And she *never* had any visitors?"

The woman behind the desk shook her head. "Not unless you count delivery people. And the thing is, she has—*had*—one of our bigger apartments. People who can afford anything on 7 or above are, well...*comfortable*, you know? They've been careful with their money. And—oh, God, this is going to sound so mean—our older residents who have a little money, they tend to get visitors. You know—family and friends who want to be left a little something in the will. Not to imply that they don't love their grandma or grandpa or great aunt or whoever, but...oh, my; I'm really putting my foot in it here, aren't I?"

"Not particularly," said Dobbs.

The woman shook her head. "But not Miss Driscoll. Never a visitor, just the deliveries. I'll bet she had two, three packages a week delivered to her. And some of those packages were fairly sizeable. On days when she had deliveries, she never came down for meals, just called the desk and said she wasn't feeling well and could she have her meals sent to her room. We do that here, send meals to a resident's room if they're not feeling good enough to come down."

"So she'd sometimes miss, what—three meals a week?"

"More, if it was a big delivery day."

I couldn't help but wonder why Dobbs was asking all these questions, unless it had something to do with what he'd told me about treating the dead with respect; maybe asking questions gave him some sense of what kind of person they had been while alive, and helped him decide how best to treat their remains.

And maybe he was just a good, old-fashioned, first-class nib-shit.

The woman behind the desk gave the freight elevator key to Dobbs. "Your gurney doesn't squeak, does it?"

"No, ma'am, it certainly does not."

She nodded her head. "That's good. I wouldn't want the other residents to be disturbed by this—at least, not any more than they already have been."

Dobbs thanked her for the key, turned to leave, then looked back. "You don't by chance know who called this in, do you?"

"I know it wasn't me, I just came on-duty a couple of hours ago, but…wait a second, please, I'll check the phone log." She called up something on her computer. "We have to keep records of who makes this kind of call, and when, all that good stuff." She found what she was looking for, scrolled up, then down, then said, "Huh."

"Something wrong?" asked Dobbs.

"There's nothing here. If the call had been made from this desk or the manager's office, it would be entered in the phone records. But…there's nothing."

"So maybe it was one of her neighbors?"

"Let me check." She called up another file, then another, then one more. "Okay, this is odd."

Dobbs gave me a quick look, then went back to the desk. "You're not gonna actually make me *ask*, are you?"

The woman looked at him, then back at the computer screen as if she expected the information she'd been searching for to have suddenly appeared during the interim. "We have certain rules that all our residents abide by, and one of those rules is that in a situation like this, if they make the call to the police, they are to immediately inform us so that we can enter it into the records. When a resident passes away on the premises, it's vital that we record every bit of information—not just for the family's peace of mind, but to protect ourselves should any legal questions arise." She looked back at Dobbs. "There's nothing here about Miss Driscoll's dying—and I mean *nothing*." Her eyes narrowed. "This is lazy and thoughtless and inexcusable. We could get into a lot of trouble for this."

"I won't say anything," said Dobbs. "But it looks like maybe this'd be a good time for you to enter some information, huh?"

"I…I don't know any of the specifics, I wouldn't know where—"

Dobbs handed her a photocopy of the forms given to him by the Coroner's Office. "Most everything's there; when we got the call, when the doc arrived here, the estimated time of death, the doc's official conclusion, all of it."

She took the forms from him. "Do you always carry extra copies of this stuff?"

"All the time. You'd be surprised how many people forget to write this stuff down when someone dies."

She pressed the forms against her chest and sighed with relief. "You're a life-saver, you know that?"

"All part of my famous curmudgeonly charm." And with a wave, he left, gesturing me to follow.

"Why all the questions?" I asked him as we re-entered the parking garage.

"You mean about Miss Driscoll?" He shrugged. "I dunno, it's just something I do on jobs like this. Seems like, since I'm gonna be the last human contact their bodies will ever know outside of a funeral home, I ought to know a little something about them. It's a terrible thing, to have your last human contact be with a total stranger. Just seems right somehow, knowing a few things." Another shrug. "Or maybe I'm just a nib-shit."

I laughed, but not too loudly.

Dobbs inserted and turned the key, pressed the button, and the freight elevator doors opened. We maneuvered the gurney into the too-wide, too-deep, too brightly-lit compartment and Dobbs pressed **7**. The doors closed with a *thump!* that seemed so loud I actually started.

"Easy there, Rambo," said Dobbs. "This ain't the time to get a case of the willies. You just follow my lead once we're up there, okay? Let me do the talking with the officer, and once we get inside, don't do a thing unless I say so, okay?"

"Okay." I sounded just as anxious as I felt.

"Hey, look at me. The first time I had to go along on one of these, I was so scared I thought I was either gonna piss my pants or throw up. I surprised myself by doing both."

"If that was meant to make me feel better, it needs a little work."

"I'm just saying that it's okay to be nervous. Do yourself a favor and don't fight it. Fighting it's what makes it worse. If it'll help, just pretend that you're moving a piece of antique furniture. I know that sounds cold-hearted as all get-out, but if you can put yourself into that frame of mind—that you're moving a thing, not a person—it'll go easier. Besides, when you get right down to it, that *is* all we're doing, moving a *thing*. It's not really a person, it's just something they once walked around in."

"Then why bother asking all those questions like you did?"

"We're not talking about *me*, Einstein, we're talking about how *you* can handle this. I've been doing this a helluva lot longer, and asking questions is how *I* deal with it so I can get to sleep at night and not feel so soul-sick and sad when I wake up the next morning that I can't get out of bed."

"I didn't mean to offend you, Fred."

"I know. And I apologize if my tone was a bit harsh. But that's my advice *for you*; if worse comes to worst, just think of them as being a piece of furniture, got it?"

I swallowed—a bit too loudly for my nerves—and nodded. "Thanks."

"Look, on an average month the Coroner's Office only gets maybe one or two calls like this. Mostly what you and me will be doing is hauling bodies from the morgue to whatever funeral home they're going to. We might have to maybe drive a body over to another county, or go to another county to bring a body back here, but mostly what we do is fill out paperwork and sit around waiting for Doc to call us with a job."

"Filling out paperwork sounds delightful right about now."

Dobbs reached across and patted my arm. "You'll be fine. Just do me a favor—you feel anything coming up or your bladder starting to do the Watusi, you make a beeline for the toilet. Oh, I forgot to mention—the first two things you locate once we're inside are, 1) the body, and, 2) the toilet. Long as you know where both of them are at all times, you should be okay."

The elevator came to a groaning stop and the doors opened. We rolled everything out into a concrete corridor, following the signs past custodian closets and storage rooms until we came to a set of heavy swinging metal doors that led into another warmly-lit hallway with gold carpeting. Its design and decor was an almost exact replica of the lobby.

According to the wall-mounted signs, 716 (Miss Driscoll's room) was to our left. We rounded the corner (making almost no noise whatsoever; Dobbs was right, this gurney was *quiet*) and the police officer sitting watch outside the room rose from her chair and gave us a nod.

"Been waiting long?" asked Dobbs when we got there.

"About forty-five minutes," said the officer, whose nametag identified her as Carol Seiler. She pushed some blonde hair back from her almost-cherubic face (the only thing marring the "cherubic" image being the heat she was packing) and said, "I guess I have to earn my salary now and ask you if you've got some official-type paperwork to show me."

Dobbs handed her the forms. She looked them over, nodded, initialed the bottom of each, took her copies, then gave back everything else.

"You've got quite the show waiting for you in there," she said.

Dobbs looked at me with an expression that was, for him, wide-eyed: *Maybe we're gonna need the sci-fi gear, after all?*

"Is it bad?" he asked.

"The body is fine, but the rest of it is…well, a little strange."

"'A little strange'?" said Dobbs. "I don't like starting my Mondays with 'strange'. Doc didn't say anything to me about 'strange.' But then, he didn't say much of *anything* to me. Don't suppose you'd care to elaborate on this 'strange'?"

Officer Seiler shook her head. "And ruin the surprise?"

By now, I was getting a serious case of the jitters; maybe these two dealt with stuff like this frequently enough that they could afford to be flippant, but my composure was just about at the breaking point.

"Could you just tell us, *please*?" I said, a bit more loudly than was probably called for.

Officer Seiler looked at me, then back at Dobbs. "Let me guess, your new CS sidekick?"

"He's a bit uneasy."

"Think maybe he's wound too tight?"

"Could be, but he seems like an okay guy."

Don't you just love having people talk about you like you're not there? Does wonders for the old self-esteem.

The two of them continued chatting about this and that—how the department was still trying to track down family members, the weather, the accident in Columbus that was all over the news, the recent budget cuts (*Damn* the budget cuts!)—so I turned around to lean against the wall and nearly jumped out of my shorts when I found myself face to face with a small, slightly hunched, bespectacled man who immediately reminded me of the drawings of Mole from *The Wind and the Willows.*

"She was an odd'n," he said, nodding toward room 716.

"Hello," I said, nothing if not quick on my feet.

"I'll not speak ill of the dead," said Mole, "but I have to tell you, I'm not going to miss the power outages."

I looked toward 716, then back at him. "Okay…?"

He gave out with one of those exasperated sighs that suggests the listener should have been able to figure out the rest for themselves already, if they had half a brain and were paying attention, which obviously I had not been so he was going to explain it to me very slowly, taking pity on my lack of common sense. "Them *packages* she was always getting. Every time she got a delivery, you could count on the power on this floor going out sometime that night. Got so bad that the management company had the custodians install a breaker box down by the laundry room so they wouldn't have to keep going to the basement. Thought it was damned considerate of them, myself. Power goes out, one of us'd just grab a flashlight, go down to the laundry room, flip a switch. Still, you couldn't stay mad at her, not hearing the way she cried some nights."

I didn't want to know this. One of my greatest fears is that I'll end up old, sick, alone, and forgotten, living out the remainder of my shabby days in some dim little room with no one to talk to or care whether or not I wake every day to the promise of more loneliness, feeling like my whole life has meant nothing.

Just spreading my sunshine. Hence the daily doses of Zoloft.

I was about to go into this woman's home and remove her body. The last goddamn thing I needed to hear was that she kept some of her neighbors awake because she cried every night. It was just too much.

"Yeah," said Mole when I made no response, "that old gal could caterwaul with the best of 'em, I swear. I mean, some nights, she'd *wail* like nobody's business." He stopped talking for a moment, something having just occurred to him. "Huh. You know, now that I think of it, it seems like the worst nights were those right after she got a big delivery." He narrowed his eyes, thinking hard, then nodded his head. "Yes sir, that'd be right. Anytime she got a big package delivered to her, you could count on two things: the power going out, and her crying up a storm. Like I said, she was an odd'n. You got any idea if someone from her family's gonna be dropping by for her stuff? Don't mean to sound morbid, but I'd sure like to get a look at whatever it was she had going on in there." This last said in a tone suggesting Miss Driscoll had some kind of juicy, dirty little secret that he was just dying to be the first to know about.

I felt even more nervous now. "I, uh…as far as I know, they're still trying to track down her family."

"Damn shame. Don't think I ever saw a visitor come to her door, aside from the delivery people."

"That's what I heard." I wanted him to go away. I was trying to think of a tactful way to tell him as much when Officer Seiler stepped in to serve and protect.

"Come on, Mr. Boyle," she said, gently taking his arm. "Let's stay out of their way so these two gentlemen can do their jobs."

"Damn shame," he said again as she led him away.

"It sure is," she replied, casting a quick glance over her shoulder and winking at me. Even packing heat, she looked so gorgeous right then I wanted to bear all of her children.

"You ready?" asked Dobbs, opening the door.

"No."

"Good answer."

We righted the gurney and rolled it into the apartment, closing the door behind us should any curious eyes decide to sneak a peek.

I found myself hoping that Officer Seiler hadn't actually left, that she'd stuck around long enough to make sure no crowd formed in the hallway, that maybe she'd thought it over and decided I was just the guy to carry her offspring.

The apartment had a small foyer with a polished wood coat rack, telephone stand, and single chair for callers to use. A framed photograph on the wall over the phone showed a very striking woman surrounded by what looked like dozens of children, all of them smiling the type of forced, could-you-*hurry*-up-and-take-the-picture-*puh-leeeeze* smile that we've all plastered on our faces at one time or another as suited the occasion. I wondered if Miss Driscoll had been a grade-school teacher at some point in her life, because all of the children in the photo looked to be between the ages of 7 and 12. The glass covering the photo was cracked, the break running down the center of the woman's face. I wondered why Miss Driscoll had never bothered replacing the glass.

"All right," said Dobbs, letting go of his end of the gurney and walking into the living room, "let me make sure we've got a clear path before we…"

"Before we what?" I asked, trying to squeeze around the gurney to join him.

"*…hol-ee shit…*"

"What is it?"

"You are *not* going to believe this."

You heard it here first.

I honesty don't know what I was expecting to see—a room filled with stuffed animals, or priceless antiques, maybe porcelain figurines of angels or those little statues of children with those really big eyes that are supposed to warm your heart but personally give me the creeps; whatever it was, it'd be something lonely-old-lady-like, that was for certain—

—I'd sure like to get a look at whatever it was she had going on in there—

—but I think even Mole a.k.a. Mr. Boyle would have started at the sight of what took up a full eighty percent of this old woman's living room.

Table-mounted HO slot-car racing tracks.

It wasn't just the sheer *amount* of track—though that in itself was enough to drop your jaw (lay all the individual pieces end to end, and my guess is you'd easily have a quarter-mile or more of the stuff)—but the configurations. These tracks weren't arranged in anything so banal as circles or ovals or figure eights, but in complex, looping, multi-layered patterns, complete with overpasses, off-ramps, and even rest areas. Model buildings were placed at various points along and around these tracks (there were a half-dozen tracks set up throughout the spacious living room) depicting small townships and bigger cities, including HO-scale trees and human figures.

"Good Christ," said Dobbs, looking around the room. "There must be about three or four thousand dollars' worth of track and… stuff."

"At least," I replied, still trying to absorb all of it. Then thought: *No wonder the power was always going out.*

The biggest track—a four-lane job—was wired for individually powered lanes, with power taps located at three different points around the track, all of the wires running underneath the table to a variable 20-amp power supply that was mounted to a small metal shelf running between two of the table's legs.

I used to be a slot-car racing *fool* when I was a kid, and I knew damn well that you can only run a power supply for *so long* before it starts to really heat up, and if you push your luck (like I always did) you were apt to blow a fuse before you were done.

And if for some reason you had *several* tracks and power supplies running at the same time…you could blow out the electricity to the entire floor of an apartment building.

I was so caught up in my own amazement that I didn't even realize Dobbs had left the living room until he came back in and said, "Oh, *man*, you gotta see the rest of this place! She's got tracks mounted *everywhere*—in her bedroom, the guest room, the kitchen…hell, she's even got a little one set up in the *bathroom!*"

"We're never going to get the gurney through here," I said. "There's barely room to walk around."

Dobbs nodded his head. "Yeah, I already figured that out. We're gonna have to move a couple of these tables. But not just yet." He squeezed past me, pressing the clipboard into my hands, heading for the door.

"Where are you going?"

"You just stay here, all right? Miss Driscoll's laid out in the bedroom, so you wait and take a look around. I don't think she's gonna mind." He stopped, then turned to face me. "I got a digital camera in my bag down in the wagon. I have *got* to take some pictures of this place. My wife'll never believe me."

I stared at him, blinked, then asked: "Why would anyone working a job like this carry a camera with them?"

He grinned. "Because every once in a while I come across something really *weird*, and my wife requires proof."

"Do you lie to her *that* much?"

"I don't like to think of it as *lying*. I…embellish. I embroider. I exaggerate."

"You lie."

"I lie. Just to keep her guessing, mind you. Believe me, after 32 years of marriage, nothing *I* do surprises her anymore, so I gotta do *something* to make it interesting for the old gal."

"So you carry a digital camera to work in case something weird comes up."

"That's it. Don't you ever fib to your wife?"

"I'm divorced."

"Oh, sorry. Well, didn't you ever fib to her when you were married?"

"Probably."

I was tempted to ask him what other weird things he'd encountered that required him to take pictures so his wife would believe him, then decided that some things were better left as mysteries.

"I'd rather not stay here by myself, Fred. Okay if I come along?"

"Sorry, my friend, but once we're on the premises, at least one of us has to be with the body at all times. Them's the rules."

"Then let me go and get the camera."

"Oh, no, sorry. I paid a pretty penny for that thing and nobody but me handles it. Look, you'll be fine. Back in a couple of minutes. Take a look around, it's pretty interesting."

And with that, he left me alone with a dead body, several thousand dollars' worth of custom-made slot-car racing track, and what felt like a solid rod of iron running from the top of my throat to the bottom of my stomach.

2

Okay, confession time: this was not the first instance of my being in a situation like this.

Back in the Neolithic Period, when I was a senior at Cedar Hill High School and working part-time for the same janitorial company I still worked for, a guy in my class by the name of Andy Leonard flipped out one Fourth of July and killed a bunch of people, including most of his family. The man who owned the company at the time—a Vietnam vet named Jackson Davies—was hired by the city to go in and clean up the Leonard house after the police were finished with it. No one who worked for him wanted to help, so he wound up offering me and a couple of other guys—Mark Sieber and Russell Brennert—300 dollars each to go in with him. Brennert had been Leonard's best friend. Mark and I gave Brennert a pretty hard time that night; hell, everyone in town was still upset and sick about the murders, and I guess we were looking for a scapegoat. Things were pretty bad in Cedar Hill for a long time after that particular July Fourth.

I will never forget what that house felt like; even from the street, you could *sense* the death that had soaked into its walls and floors. Once inside, that death got on your own skin, as well.

And it was so cold. I don't think I've ever been that cold in my life. I couldn't stop shaking the whole time we were in there.

I don't know if it's possible to put into words how it feels to mop up a puddle of blood and tissue that used to be a human being. Sometimes I still have nightmares about it.

Brennert wound up going into the nuthouse for a few weeks after that night. After we graduated, he kept on working for Davies until

Davies decided to retire to Florida. Brennert bought the company from him. It said an awful lot about Brennert's character that he hired me right on the spot when I came looking for work after both college and my marriage (in that order) didn't work out. We never talk about that night. I guess we can still smell that cold, cold death on each other. Like I could smell it now. Hence the rod of iron inside me.

Since I couldn't just *stand* there—it seemed like there were shadows in every corner trying to move in around me—I heeded Dobbs' advice and took a walking tour of the place.

Altogether, Miss Driscoll had 17 tracks of various sizes mounted throughout her apartment—though the track in the bathroom, a small, simple oval, was a battery-operated child's version of what engulfed the rest of the place. She had arranged the larger tracks to create aisles so that she could move easily between rooms. I couldn't help but wonder at her fascination with these things.

And then thought of her loneliness.

Everything told you that this wasn't just a hobby with this woman, it was an obsession, something she'd fostered to fill the holes in her life. Dobbs might have found this interesting in a weird sort of way, but the more I moved from room to room, seeing the *details* she'd added to each setup (tiny bits of trash spilling from a trash can at a rest stop; the tired, road-weary expressions on the peoples' faces; a vending machine with an **Out Of Order** sign taped to its front), the more it all struck me as frighteningly sad. A lot of *care* had gone into the construction and maintenance of these tracks, and I couldn't help but wonder if it had been her way of avoiding her loneliness.

It was in the guest bedroom that I first began to notice the trashed cars and tiny memorial wreaths set among the HO-scale buildings. The trashed cars were bad enough—how she'd managed to crumple some of these like she had was beyond me, but *damn* if they didn't look like the real thing—but it was the miniature wreaths and crosses that really started to unnerve me. You've seen the real thing, I'm sure: drive for any length of time on any stretch of highway through any state, and you'll pass them; sad little shrines—some homemade, others bought from florist shops—left behind by family members and friends to mark the place where someone they loved died in an automobile accident. Crosses and hearts seem to be the two most popular shapes, usually constructed of wire mesh covered in plastic flowers or plastic white lace to make the shape stand out, ribbons hand-tied all around to flutter in the breeze as if that silent activity was meant to fill the world with movements the dead could no longer make for themselves…and always, in the center of these memorials, staring out at passing cars whose drivers never return the eye contact, are the photographs, the faces of those who will never again see a new place, a different road, or a light in the window waiting for them at journey's end.

Yes, give me a mondo case of the willies and I turn into a half-assed poet.

All of the tiny wreaths and crosses that were set at various points around the tracks had even tinier photographs in their centers.

And each one was numbered on the back.

I got out of there, found myself in the suddenly too-small hallway, and without thinking about it walked through the nearest doorway—

—and right into Miss Driscoll's bedroom.

To this day I don't know why I didn't just turn around and leave once I realized where I was. I could have just waited in the living room for Dobbs to come back, but I guess morbid curiosity got the better of me.

The thing is, her body was the *last* thing I noticed.

Expensive track lighting ran along opposite sides of the room, giving the place the too-bright look of a department store; if you wanted to make sure you kept yourself awake at night, this was the way to do it. There were two table-mounted tracks in here, and they were even more intricate than the others—one of them was a four-lane triple-tiered job that must have taken *days* to set up. There was a computer that had an LCD flat-screen monitor bigger than my television. Pages torn from what looked like a few dozen road and highway atlases were taped to the walls, the windows, and her dresser mirror. The pages sparkled under the harsh lighting, and it was only as I moved closer to a few of them that I saw why: the maps were decorated with dozens, hundreds, maybe even *thousands* of small foil stars, each roughly the size of my thumbnail. (Remember those little stars that your kindergarten teacher would stick on your drawings when you got an "A"? Yeah, *those*.) They were all over these maps; some of the stars were silver, some of them were blue, but most of them were gold.

And each one had a hand-written number in its center.

Out in the hallway, a shadow moved near the door.

"Fred?" I called out.

Nothing. My imagination. My nerves.

I was getting jumpy. *Jumpier*.

Stepping back, I moved to the side in an effort to avoid bumping into one of the tracks and in the process banged my hip into the back of the desk chair, that in turn rolled forward, hit the keyboard tray, and woke the machine from Sleep mode.

There were two images displayed side by side on the screen: one was the schematic of an HO-track configuration; the second was a map of the I-71 loop in Columbus.

They were the same shape. I knew this because I'd just seen it.

It was behind me.

I turned to look at the second table-mounted track and, sure enough, eight mashed cars had been set aside, and seven small memorials had been placed at the spot where the accident had occurred.

Not being one whose grasp of the obvious will ever be called keen, I looked back at the computer screen, then again at the track, then once more at the computer.

Which is when I finally noticed the stack of files beside the desk.

Another shadow, this one bulkier than the last, moved in the periphery of my vision. I stomped to the doorway and looked in every direction but saw no further movement.

"Fred? Goddammit, *c'mon*, this isn't funny."

No answer. No sound.

Checking my watch, I saw that Dobbs had been gone only three minutes. It felt like I'd been alone in here for hours.

Ever had one of those "I-Know-This-Isn't-A-Good-Idea-*But*" moments?

The smart thing to do was leave the room and not look at anything else.

The smart thing to do was leave.

Once more, with feeling: Smart Thing = Leaving.

So of course I turned back, picked up the top file, and sat down in the desk chair to look at it.

It was a record of traffic deaths.

The first several pages consisted of hand-written columns noting dates, locations, number and makes of cars, fatalities, and the names of everyone involved. Next to each line of information was a number written in blue, silver, or gold ink. The rest of the file contained newspaper clippings, arranged by date, containing details (and sometimes photos) about the accidents catalogued in the first batch of pages.

Closing the file and setting it back atop the stack, I looked around the bedroom once more.

How goddamn lonely, bitter, angry, and *morbid* would someone have to be to make this their *hobby?* I mean, it was bad enough she'd spent so much time collecting and organizing this information, but to drop thousands of dollars on custom-made HO track and accessories to *recreate* the accidents in the privacy of her home…can I get an *Eeeewwww!*?

And to top it all off, she hadn't even gotten the last accident right; *five* people, not seven, had died as a result of the I-71 crash.

I stood, pulling my wallet from my back pocket and thumbing through its contents until I found my lawyer's business card. I wanted out of this. If it meant some jail time instead of community service, so be it. I was so creeped out that even the threat of incarceration seemed preferable to spending one more minute in this apartment. Brennert would understand. I wouldn't lose my job over this. He was that kind of guy. (And I had serious doubts that the judge would actually put me in jail; I'd probably end up washing dishes at the Open Shelter or something like that.)

I spotted the phone among the stuff on the cluttered nightstand, walked over, picked up the receiver, and only then allowed myself to look down at Miss Driscoll's body.

She *might* have been the same woman in the photo hanging in the foyer, but I couldn't be certain; at least fifty years separated the face in the picture from the one I was looking at now.

Staring down at her still form that looked more asleep than dead, I couldn't help but wonder how she came to this, what led from point A to point B (and so on) to her cutting herself off from the rest of the world with only this grotesque hobby to fill her days.

Is that why you cried some nights? I wondered. *Did you know or suspect that your life had become something ghoulish and ugly? Did you feel so powerless and alone and afraid that you couldn't talk to someone about it? Did it hurt* that *much, knowing what you had become?*

"Lady," I whispered, "what the hell happened to you?"

I reached down with a shaking hand to punch in my lawyer's phone number and accidentally hit the **Redial** button, freezing just long enough for the seven digits to complete their rapid-fire dialing and hear a voice on the other end say: "Cedar Hill Police Department, how may I direct your call?"

"Sorry, misdialed." I hung up with too much force, just about tipping over the mostly empty glass of water next to the phone. Steadying the glass, I managed to knock one of the prescription containers from the nightstand. Sometimes I'm so graceful it's a wonder I didn't pursue a career in ballet.

Counting the one I'd knocked to the floor, there were seven empty prescription containers on the nightstand: painkillers, sedatives, blood pressure medication, muscle relaxants, antidepressants, and two different kinds of sleeping pills. There was also a good-sized bowl with remnants of chocolate pudding clinging to its rim and to the spoon lying inside (having consumed more than my fair share of chocolate pudding *and* knowing how it looks when you fail to rinse out the bowl in a timely manner, I recognized this immediately, perceptive and clever fellow—not to mention tidy housekeeper—that I am). Mixed in with these remnants was a not-so-fine powdery substance.

Oh, shit.

I take in pill form a drug called Imitrex for my migraine headaches. The stuff works wonders most of the time, except on those nights I forget to carry some on me and end up at the ER getting a shot of Demerol so I can be arrested for DUI on my way home and be assigned community service that will lead me to be standing over the dead body of a seriously weird old lady, but I digress. If I do not take the Imitrex with food or milk, I will be vomiting within half an hour. Since it takes two pills to tackle one of my migraines, I break them up into several pieces and mix them in with applesauce or— drum-roll please—pudding.

I stared at the bowl, the empty prescription containers, and knew.

Miss Driscoll had committed suicide.

Now before you shake your head and let fly with one of those long, low-pitched, boy-has-*he*-lost-it whistles, consider: 1) This was an isolated and terribly lonely old woman who, 2) had a morbid hobby, 3) possessed enough prescription medications to kill herself three times over if she took them all at once, and whose, 4) last phone call had been to the *non-emergency* number of the police department.

It would have been simple enough; wait until you feel yourself starting to drift toward sleep, then make the call: *I'm sorry, this isn't an emergency, it's probably nothing, but I live over at The Maples on—oh, you know where that is? I was wondering if you could send some officers over to apartment 716 sometime tonight around, oh, 8:30 or 9? There's a young man who's been coming to my door at that time for the last couple of nights—I think he might be trying to sell something—and he will* not *leave me alone. He's been very insistent, and he's starting to frighten me a little. I was hoping the officers might have a word with him?*

She'd probably invented a better reason, but my guess was it had been something along similar lines, some vague, borderline silly, old-lady reason to have a couple of officers drop by, nothing urgent, mind you, but allowing for enough time between the call and their visit to make sure she'd be dead when the police arrived.

I can't say that I was pleased about realizing this—consider the circumstances—because if it were true, then it raised more questions than it answered: why was there no record of this downstairs? The police would have checked in with whomever worked the front desk. The door to the apartment hadn't been forcibly opened, it had been unlocked by someone with a passkey (presumably the building manager or one of the security guards). How did the mayor come to be involved? And why would the coroner file a false report of "Natural Causes" when it must have been obvious to him that Miss Driscoll had taken her own life? (C'mon; if I could figure it out based on an almost-empty pudding bowl, someone with the coroner's medical knowledge must have known it the moment he saw the body.)

Two things stopped me from deciding that I was full of shit and just letting my anxiety get the better of me; the first was something Dobbs had said on the way over here: "…this whole to-do was *supposed* to be handled by the book, but there ain't been nothing about this has gone like it's *supposed* to."

The second thing was what I saw when I finally worked up enough nerve to test my theory and picked up the bowl: pieces of pills mixed in with the remaining glops of pudding.

Now what was I supposed to do?

First thing: put down the bowl.

The second thing was what I should have done in the first place—get the hell out of the room. I'd put in my CS time today, go home, and call my lawyer this evening. Whatever was going on here was out of my hands and none of my business.

Hell, yes, I felt bad for Miss Driscoll—you'd have to be a monster not to—but none of this was my responsibility. A lonely old lady offs herself and some city officials decide for whatever reason to cover it up. Fine. I was just here to transport her body so she could get some kind of decent burial. And like Dobbs had said, ultimately this wasn't *her*, it was just something she used to walk around in. Wherever she was now (assuming there *was* a Wherever), she had better things to concern herself with.

"I see you've located the body," said Dobbs from the doorway.

I looked over just in time to be half-blinded by the sudden flash of his camera.

"Oh, *man*, you ought to see the expression on your face. " He started over, working his way around the tracks. "Take a gander." He turned the camera's display window toward me.

"All I can see right now are spots."

"Oh, sorry about that. I couldn't resist."

If I was going to say anything about this, now was my chance. I pointed at the cluttered bedside table. "You notice anything odd?"

Dobbs looked at the table. "She was a bit messy."

"Is that all?"

He shrugged. "I dunno. What am I supposed to be seeing?"

"Humor me. Take a good look at what's on this table."

Dobbs sighed, then leaned down to examine everything. He picked up the pudding bowl, stared at its contents, and made the Stroke Face again, so I knew he was concentrating.

After several seconds, he said: "Gimme the clipboard."

I handed it over and he flipped through the official paperwork.

"Son-of-a-bitch," he whispered.

"What?"

He looked down at Miss Driscoll, then at me. "You first."

I shook my head. "Oh, no. No. Sorry but…no. I don't want to get myself in any more trouble than I already am."

Dobbs stared at me, blinked, then nodded. "She died of natural causes like my ass chews gum."

"So…what do we do about it?"

Dobbs looked back at Miss Driscoll's body, then rubbed his eyes. "Nothing, that's what. We don't do a goddamn *thing* about it. If the doc falsified the report, I'm guessing it's because the mayor *told* him to."

"But aren't you curious to know why?"

"*Shit*, yes—but I'm also…" He shook his head. "Look, we say anything about this to the doc or the mayor or anyone official, there's going to be a lot of questions, then some kind of investigation, and all sorts of nasty shit for us to deal with. Maybe it don't make any difference to you, you're only here temporary, but me, I gotta think about my *job*, you understand? If a city employee makes any kind of an accusation against a city official, then they'd better have some goddamn *proof* or else they're gonna be out on their unemployed ass in a hurry. You got any medical background? *I* sure as hell don't. Who do you think people would believe, anyway—the County Coroner or a couple of schleps who drive the meat wagon?"

"You could take a picture of the table, we could show that to someone, and—"

"—and how would we prove that we didn't just put all this stuff here to make it *look* like she offed herself? You know as well as I do that someone would think that."

"We call the Columbus police department, get them to send over someone from their lab, they could—"

"Are you *listening* to yourself? First of all, that kind of call would have to come from the mayor, the sheriff, the chief of police, or the coroner. Second, even if you and me *did* call and somehow managed to get them to come, we'd have to sit here with the body until they arrived—and I don't know about you, but I don't feel like babysitting a corpse for however long it'd take them to get here. And *third*, how do you suppose they'd react once they dusted this place and found our fingerprints—" He pointed to the pudding bowl. "—on what is probably the central piece of evidence?"

As soon as he pointed at the pudding bowl, something occurred to me. "Why is this stuff still here?"

"Say what?"

I nodded at everything on the bedside table. "If the doc and the mayor have decided to cover this up, at least *on paper*, then why not get rid of the evidence, as well? Why leave all of this stuff out in plain view and risk someone being able to figure it out?"

"They couldn't be sure that somebody *would*, maybe?"

I shook my head. "No—c'mon, Fred. *I* figured it out. If it'd been you up here instead of me, *you* would've noticed something, too. It's almost like…"

"Like what?"

I looked back up at him. "It's like somebody *wanted* you and me to figure it out."

"But why?"

I shrugged. "Beats the hell out of me."

"There you go, then," said Dobbs. "Maybe there's something to what you're saying, okay? *Maybe*. But if you're right, if they did leave all this shit out hoping that we'd put two and two together, how're they gonna know unless we say something? If we don't do anything, if we don't *say* anything, just come in here and haul her body away like we're supposed to, then there's no way anyone'll ever know. As long as we keep this to ourselves, it's fine."

"We can't just do *nothing*."

"The hell we can't! Listen to me, the next time we go on a call like this, you don't touch *nothing* besides the front door, the gurney, and the body, got it? We find anything weird like this again and I invite you to take a look around, just hit me, okay? I'm not that far away from collecting my pension, and I'll be *damned* if I'm gonna have it fucked up for me by a CS temp! So from now on, you don't touch *nothing* unless I say so."

There wasn't going to *be* a next time for me, so I nodded my head and muttered apologies.

Dobbs stared at me for a few more seconds, his features softening. "I don't mean to yell at you, I'm sorry. But it's a done deal at this point, all the paperwork's been filed, and the best thing that you and me can do is just...what we came here to do."

"I understand."

"*Do* you?"

"Yeah. She's gone, nothing we do is going to change that, and I'd rather not be the one responsible for you losing your pension."

He reached over and gave my shoulder a little squeeze. "There's a good fellah. Me and you, we won't talk about this again, right?"

"Right."

"Or mention it to anybody else?"

"Or mention it to anybody else."

He looked around at the tracks and computer. "Still, you gotta wonder what the hell she was doing in here, all by herself, with this crap."

I pointed toward his digital camera. "Did you get enough pictures?"

He nodded. "I pretty much got the whole place before I came in here. I'm surprised you didn't hear me banging around out there."

"I was, uh..." I looked at Miss Driscoll's bedside table. "...a little preoccupied."

"I heard that." He looked at me and smiled. "C'mon. Let's go clear a path so we can get the gurney in here."

It took us over half an hour to move the tracks, and even then it was a tight squeeze, but somehow we managed. We lifted Miss Driscoll's body from the bed (she didn't weigh very much, I could have done it alone), put her inside the bag, and zipped it closed.

There was a cold finality in that sound that, for a moment, put me back inside the Leonard house.

Christ, I didn't want to be here.

Dobbs took the lead. We'd gotten the gurney almost all the way to the foyer when one of the wheels on his end locked up.

"Son-of-a…hold on a second, will you?"

"Sure thing." I let go of my end, stood there for a moment, and then noticed something. "Hey, Fred, do you have the clipboard?"

"No," he said from somewhere below the gurney. "What'd we do, leave it in the bedroom?"

"Looks like."

His head came around the far right wheel leg. "*Well?*"

I looked at him.

He looked back at me, then sighed. "Hey, here's a question—when you were going to school, did you ride there on a long bus or a short one?"

"So you're saying I should go back and get it."

"Whatta *you* think?"

"I think I'll go back and get it."

His head disappeared behind the gurney leg once more. "I'm so proud right now."

Back in the bedroom, I found the clipboard lying on the floor in front of the bedside table. I retrieved it and started making my way out of the room when I gave into a sudden impulse, turned back, and removed one of the numerous star-covered maps from the wall. Folding it up and slipping it into my back pocket, I went back to help Dobbs move the gurney out into the foyer.

"You doing okay?" he asked once we were back in the hall.

"I guess."

Dobbs pulled the door to 716 closed, checking to make sure it locked behind him, then said, "You look kinda upset to me."

"This hasn't been the best morning. Could we just *go*, please?"

We began moving the gurney toward the end of the hall. Dobbs asked, "So…think you're gonna have the stomach for this?"

"I haven't urped on your shoes yet, have I?"

"Just checking. Usually with CS temps, this is about the time most of them decide they'd rather risk roadside trash pickup, dishwashing, or jail. But all things considered, you held your own real good here this morning."

"Thanks." And I meant it. Dobbs didn't strike me as the kind of guy who was in the habit of handing out compliments like business cards at a convention, so knowing that I'd earned his seal of approval actually made me feel kind of proud of myself.

"I have decided," said Dobbs, "that you *aren't* okay, that you're just trying to put up a good front for me. I have decided that this kind of stiff-upper-lip behavior deserves rewarding. I have decided that you need cheering up."

"Oh, you have, have you?"

"Yes, and since I'm in charge, you're getting cheered up. Besides, I'm hungry."

We were just turning the corner at the end of the hall when I chanced a look back at Miss Driscoll's apartment and saw a bulky shadow closing the door from the inside. A second later, the deadbolt was engaged. I started to say something to Dobbs, then changed my mind; after all, we didn't see anything suspicious, did we?

3

We headed for a nearby McDonald's. Since Dobbs wanted to avoid the crowd inside (and the thought of leaving Miss Driscoll's body unattended seemed—to me, anyway—creepier than our eating our lunch while sitting in the wagon with it), we placed our orders at the drive-thru.

The people in the cars in front of and behind us kept looking at the wagon and trying to look like they weren't looking. Hard to miss a big-ass white wagon with the word **CORONER** written across the back and sides (as well as backwards across the front).

Because Dobbs was picky about how his food was to be prepared (so it was going to take a few extra minutes), we were asked to pull out of line and go wait in one of the parking spaces designated **Drive-Thru Customers Only**.

So we sat there while the rest of the customers took their bags of food and kept looking over.

Two other cars were asked to move out of line and park in our area, which they did, one on either side of us. It was a hot day and everyone—including Dobbs and me—had our windows rolled down.

There were two windows in the rear doors of the wagon, and one on either side toward the back. These side windows came equipped with blinds that could be lowered so as to keep the body from view of passing drivers.

Dobbs had forgotten to lower the side blinds, so the cars parked on either side of us had a clear, unobstructed view of the bagged body.

The man and little girl in the car on Dobbs' side looked about half sick.

The young woman in the car on my side sat with her hands on the steering wheel, staring straight out at the patch of weeds beyond the parking lot.

Dobbs finally turned to face the man and little girl on his side. He raised his hand and gave a short wave. "Hi'ya."

"Hey," said the little girl.

"Elizabeth," said her father, "don't bother the…nice man."

"Oh, she ain't botherin' me," Dobbs replied. "We're just waiting on our order."

"Me, too," said the little girl. Then: "Is that a dead person back there?"

"Sure is."

"What'cha doin' with it?"

"Just making a delivery."

The man turned ashen, but the woman sitting in the car on my side was red-faced.

The little girl asked, "Where you taking the body?"

Dobbs smiled. "That's a secret."

The little girl looked from Dobbs to the body, then at the golden arches.

The woman in the car next to me made a sound, and I looked over to see her lowering her head, her lips pressed tightly together but quivering; she was trying so hard not to laugh.

About this time, a young woman looking shapely and cute in her Mickey-D's uniform came out with our order, handing it through the window to Dobbs. "Here's your order, sir. Thank you for your patience."

“No problem,” said Dobbs. Then: “So, which door in the back do we go to?”

“I beg your pardon, sir?” She looked at him for a moment, then rolled her eyes and sighed. “Oh, no, not *you* again…”

Dobbs started the engine. “Yes, me again. Now, which door? We go through this every time, and I, for one, am getting bored with this little innocent routine you insist on playing. This stuff won’t stay fresh for long, not in this weather.”

The woman in the car next to me looked like she might burst a vein in her head if she held her laughter in much longer.

“Never mind,” said Dobbs to the Mickey-D’s crewperson. “I understand, all these witnesses and everything.” He winked at her. “We’ll find it.”

The young woman slunk back inside, shaking her head and muttering.

Dobbs pulled his Quarter Pounder out of the bag, unwrapped it, lifted the top part of the bun to check it, and then shrieked. Everyone else—including me—jumped at the sound.

“Oh, my God!” said Dobbs. “It’s true. *God help us all, it’s true!*”

He backed out then, shouting, *“Soylent Green is people! Soylent Green is people! Soylent Green is peeeeeeeeeeeeeeople!”*

The man in the other car gripped the steering wheel and placed his forehead against the backs of his hands. His daughter was jumping up and down, shouting *“Soylent Green is people!”* The woman in the farthest car was howling with laughter, and customers inside were lining the windows, staring.

Dobbs stopped at the exit, opened his door, and—brandishing his Quarter Pounder like it was the Olympic torch—stood up on the running board: *"I can't take it anymore! I warn you all—fear the Mystery Meat! Fear it! Fear it! For the love of all that's good and decent, FEAR IT!"* Then he got back inside the wagon and drove away as if nothing had happened.

After we were back on the road, I said: "You're a very weird person, Dobbs."

"But not *boring*. Gotta give me that much."

"What about your pension? Won't you get into trouble if someone calls to complain?"

"I haven't yet. I pull this routine every time I get a new CS sidekick. Consider it your initiation."

"I thought the idea was to cheer me up."

Dobbs shrugged. "Actually, the idea was to cheer *me* up. You were turning into a real Gloomy Gus."

I figured I wouldn't be going back to that particular McDonald's anytime soon.

The rest of the day wasn't nearly as interesting.

We took Miss Driscoll to the morgue, filled out the paperwork, then read over our orders for the rest of the afternoon: taking a body from the morgue to the Henderson Funeral Home (then more paperwork), picking up another body from the nursing home and transporting it directly to Criss Brothers' Funeral Home (two different sets of paperwork on that one), topped off with moving a third body from Criss Brothers' *to* Henderson's because of a screw-up with someone else's paperwork. (We never did get that one figured out, so no paperwork for us. Hoo. Ray.)

When I got home that night, there were three messages: the first was from Russell Brennert, assuring me once again that my job was safe, not to worry, my crew was doing fine, he'd checked up on them himself, and if I wanted to switch shifts to get in some evening hours during my CS period, he'd be more than happy to arrange it; the second message was from one of my crew members, telling me that things had gone okay and everyone was wondering if I'd still be handing out the paychecks at the end of the month or if they'd have to go to the office for them; and the last message was from Barbara Greer, my lawyer.

"Meet me for breakfast at the Sparta tomorrow morning. 8:30. It's important."

I've known Barb since high school. She used to date Andy Leonard. Like Brennert, she'd endured no end of suspicion and abuse from people during the months and years after the murders. And also like Brennert, she and I have never once discussed what happened that night.

Barb is not a person who talks in short sentences; she tends to preface things, give details, and lean toward excessive small talk, even when leaving phone messages. (I've always suspected that silence makes her uncomfortable, hence her always keeping the conversation going.)

There was a tension in her voice that I hadn't heard since the murders.

And she used short sentences.

And she hadn't asked me to meet her, she'd *told* me to. (Barb never *orders* anyone. Never.)

Whatever was going on, it *must* be important. She knew I had to be in the meat wagon with Dobbs by nine a.m. sharp, and if the traffic was on my side I could make it from the Sparta to the coroner's office in about 15 minutes.

I fixed myself some microwave macaroni and cheese, popped open a soda, and watched a Cary Grant movie called *People Will Talk* that had one of those happy endings that leaves you with a lump in your throat. After that I washed the dishes, read the paper, then went to bed.

Yes, it's a full life I lead.

4

"Where is it?"

Opening my eyes, I saw the digital clock on my bedside table.

4:42 a.m.

The voice from my dream was fading. I sighed, rolled onto my back, and started to drift off once more when a hand I could have sat in clamped around my neck and began to squeeze.

"Where is it?"

I opened my eyes and saw two bulky shadows leaning over my bed. One of them pressed down, increasing its grip around my neck. The pressure was enough to hurt me but not completely cut off my breathing.

"I'll ask you one more time," said this shadow, "and then we're going to hurt you."

I struggled against the grip but it did no good. "Where's *what?*" I managed to get out.

"The map you stole from Road Mama's apartment."

Road Mama?

Okay, I was still dreaming. Cool. Not quite so scared shitless now.

"In the back pocket of my jeans. On the chair over in the corner."

"You shouldn't have stolen it, you know."

Strange, how your conscience works on you. All day long I'd felt bad about taking that damned thing.

One of the dream-shadows moved away from the bed. I heard some rustling, then: "Got it."

The pressure was released from around my neck as the second shadow let go to remove something from its pocket. "You have no idea what you've gotten yourself into." It leaned down once again, and I felt a short sting in my right arm, and then everything got warm and shiny and I rode the high back down into sleep.

When the alarm went off, I stumbled out of bed, dry-mouthed, groggy, arms and legs feeling like rubber, and grabbed my jeans from the chair in the corner.

The map was gone.

For several seconds, I was afraid to breathe.

Then I got angry, grabbing a baseball bat from the closet and stomping through the apartment in only my underwear, kicking open doors, ripping aside the shower curtain, shouting curses and promises of broken kneecaps.

Then I noticed that the deadbolt and security chain were still in place.

I made another macho-man sweep of the apartment, at one point opening the *refrigerator door* to make sure no one was hiding in there (yes, I know…), and finally deciding that I just wanted to get the hell out.

Check the other *pocket, you idiot.*

Back in the bedroom, I grabbed my jeans and checked *all* the pockets.

No map.

So if it wasn't a dream, how in hell did they get in? (And, for that matter, how did they *leave*?)

Just to make certain, I checked the front door—locked; I checked all the windows—locked; the sliding glass doors that opened onto the patio in back—locked; the refrigerator again—I needed to buy groceries.

I stood in the middle of the kitchen, tapping the business end of the bat against the side of my leg and shaking.

Maybe it was *a dream*, I thought. Sure, a dream brought on by an overly-scrupulous conscience. Maybe you took the map out of your pocket and put it somewhere else and *that's* why it isn't in your jeans.

I went to the front door and stood there, facing the inside of the apartment. I hadn't done all that much when I got home last night, so it would be easy to retrace my steps.

Front door. Bathroom. Kitchen. Living room. Bedroom.

Still no star-spackled map.

I retraced my steps again.

Nothing.

I tried it once more, this time checking between and under the couch cushions, then under the couch itself, then under the coffee table, under the bed, under the dresser, and—just for good measure—inside the refrigerator once again, where I discovered that no groceries had magically appeared, nor had the map.

"It fell out of your pocket before you got home," I said aloud, hoping the sound of my own voice would calm me. "Yeah…it fell out of your pocket somewhere along the line after you left Miss Driscoll's apartment. That's all there is to it."

I felt completely silly now.

I continued to feel silly all the way through coffee, my shower, and getting dressed. Driving to the Sparta, the feeling of silliness gave way to mild gaiety, and by the time I walked into the restaurant and located Barb's table, I was dangerously close to whimsical.

That all came to a crashing halt when I sat down and Barb spoke.

5

"Did you give them the map?"

I felt the blood drain from my face. She *couldn't* have said what I thought she'd said. I asked her to repeat the question.

Leaning forward, she nailed me to the spot with her piercing green eyes and said: "Did you give them the map?"

Shit, shit, shit.

"Did I give who what map?"

"Don't be cute with me. Answer the question."

My heart pounded. "How did you know?"

She sat back, sighed, and reached for her coffee. "The mayor told me."

"The mayor? How the hell did he—"

"Did you give it to them?"

"First of all, if you know who 'they' are, could you let *me* in on it? We didn't exchange many pleasantries so introductions were just sort of skipped over, and second, yes, I gave it to them—or, rather, they *took* it after I told them where it was. And by the way, one of them was choking me at the time, then he gave me a shot to knock me out. And for the record, Counselor, they somehow managed to get in and out of my apartment without breaking any locks or windows, which prompts me to ask: *Jee-zus*, Barb, what's going on?"

She opened the menu and began perusing the selections. "I'm not sure."

I stared. "You never could lie worth a damn."

She shrugged. "Have it your way."

I reached over and pulled down the menu she was holding. "Is this what was so important? That stupid map? You could have asked about that in the message and had me call you back."

"No, this isn't *just* about the map—though that's part of it. Don't ask me how you managed to do it, Prince Charming, but you've gotten some very powerful people upset with you."

"What powerful people?"

"Powerful enough that both the mayor and chief of police are scared of them. Beyond that, I honestly *don't know*, okay?"

The waitress came to our table and poured coffee, took Barb's order, then asked what I'd like to have.

"I just have time for coffee," I said, looking at my watch.

Barb said, "You've got time for breakfast."

"I have to be at the coroner's office by nine."

She shook her head. "Not today, you don't. Today, you have a new community service assignment. Now order some real food. I'm guessing your diet still consists of whatever pre-packaged trans-fatty caloric nightmare you can toss into a microwave. Hopefully some real cooking won't send your system into cataleptic shock."

I ordered my breakfast and the waitress left us with a bright smile.

"Why am I here, Barb?"

"The mayor didn't call just me, he also called the coroner and Judge Banks. I spoke with Banks this morning before I came here." She produced a thick envelope from her briefcase and tossed it on the table. "This would be for you."

Inside was a Triple-A TripTik, a sheet of paper with street directions, an address, and a phone number written on it, as well as three hundred dollars in fifties and a cashier's check made out to me in the sum of one thousand dollars.

"What gives? Is this check for real?"

Barb added some sugar to her coffee. "Yes, it's for real—in fact, you can waltz your ass over to the Park National Bank right after breakfast and cash it—*if* you agree to the offer I've been authorized to make to you."

"Which is…?"

"How would you like to have your record wiped clean and fulfill all your required community service time over the next couple of days?"

I almost laughed. "Who do I have to kill?"

She blanched. "That's not funny."

"Sorry."

Barb stared at me for a moment, then shook her head. "No, *I'm* sorry. Guess I'm a little grouchy this morning."

"Apology accepted. Now, I believe there was something said at the outset about an offer…?"

"It turns out Miss Driscoll *does* have some family, and they'd like to bury her in the family plot, and they'd like her body to be driven home as soon as possible. So here's the off—you're way ahead of me, aren't you?"

I lifted the envelope. "I drive her body home, and when I get back my record is clean and my community service time is done, right?"

She nodded. "*And* you'll be two thousand dollars richer."

"Two? But the check's for—"

"I *know* how much the check is for, thank you, *I'm* the one who had it drawn up. You'll be given another one just like it when you get back. If you accept the offer, you'll have to leave today. The family wants her there by tomorrow afternoon."

I checked the directions and the TripTik. "This is an 18-hour drive. And *that's* if you go at it without having to stop."

"So you stop for gas and food when you need to, and a motel when you get tired. The cash is to cover your travel expenses."

"Just pull into my friendly Motel 6 with a stiff in the back of my car? You gotta be kidding! How am I supposed to explain a dead body if I get pulled over by the cops?"

She produced another envelope from her briefcase. "This is what's called a Federal Remains Transportation Permit. Don't be surprised if you've never heard of it, these aren't issued very often. It allows whomever is in possession of it to transport readied remains across however many state lines necessary in order to reach its intended place of interment."

I looked at her, blinked, then said: *"In English?"*

"It's a permission slip from the Federal Marshal's Office saying that it's okay for you, an Average Joe, to be driving a burial-ready stiff halfway across the country so the family can give it a proper funeral."

"Oh."

"There's usually a hell of a lot more paperwork to deal with when something like this has to be done, but Miss Driscoll's family evidently has a *lot* of pull in Washington. Neither the mayor nor the police chief would tell me who called them, or what was said, but to give you some idea of just how important someone has to be in order to rate one of these puppies, out of all the FRTPs issued since 1945, *counting* the one you're looking at—and there haven't been as many issued as you would think—one of them was to Eleanor Roosevelt so she could take FDR's body home by train."

"…holy shit."

"Tell me about it. I don't know who Miss Driscoll was, but her family has enough power to bypass every inch of local, state, and federal red tape. You don't say no to people like that."

"What if I do?"

"But why *would* you? Think about it—this is a gravy job! You'll be on the road maybe a total of two days, and when you get back home, you're a couple of grand richer *plus* your record's clean and your community service time is marked as fulfilled."

"Who wanted the map, Barb? Who wanted the map bad enough to somehow break into my apartment in the middle of the night without opening a window or a door? They *threatened* me! One of them had his big-ass hand *around my throat!* They *drugged* me, for chrissakes!"

"They're also paying you two thousand dollars to make the trip."

"Oh, well, that makes *all* the difference then, doesn't it?"

"Keep your voice down."

I took a breath, held it, and counted to ten. "Since you know about the map, then you must know what else was in her apartment, right?"

"No—and I don't *want* to know, got it? I have, as of right now, told you everything I know about this, okay?"

"Fine." I stared at the envelopes, thought about the bills I could pay off with two thousand dollars, then slid everything back across the table. "Afraid I'm going to have to pass, but *thanks*." I started to get up to leave; her hand shot out and grabbed my wrist.

"You're not leaving me stuck with the check for a meal you didn't eat. *Sit down.*"

You would have to have known her since high school to recognize the hint of fear crowding at the edges of her voice. Barbara Greer was nothing if not always in control of herself. She wasn't telling me to stay and eat; she was scared—scratch that, she was *terrified*—that I was going to walk out on the offer.

I sat back down. "I guess I *should* eat what I ordered."

"That's almost sensible, coming from you." The control was back in her voice, but behind her eyes something was shaking with near panic. She took out a pen and began scribbling something on the back of the first envelope. "I never understood how you managed to stay alive, what with the crap you eat. Do you get *any* protein besides peanut butter? Don't answer that—it would probably just depress me."

She slid the envelope toward me, all the while chatting away about this and that and nothing in particular and blah-blah-blah…

Her note read: *You don't have a choice. I can't say that out loud. People are listening.*

I looked up at her, then gestured for her pen.

You're serious, aren't you?

I pushed the envelope back to her. She read it, looked at me, and nodded her head.

"So," I said a bit too loudly, "this, uh...this deal you're offering me."

"The one you just offhandedly turned down? The one that any person in his right mind would have jumped at? *That* deal?"

"You're going to make me grovel, aren't you?"

"You were a royal horse's ass. *Yes*, I'm going to make you grovel."

"Okay—this is me, groveling. Grovel, grovel, grovel, I am an ungrateful butt-wipe, please forgive me, I am not worthy."

"Are you quite finished?"

"Grovel, grovel." I waited a moment, then said: "All done. Have I groveled enough?"

"For now."

"I've reconsidered things."

"I'll bet you have."

"I'll do it."

The look of massive relief on her face almost broke my heart. She reached across the table and squeezed my hand, not saying a word.

For the second time that morning, I was almost afraid to breathe. I kept seeing those hulking shadowed figures over my bed, one of them whispering, *You have no idea what you've gotten yourself into....*

I'd figured on having an hour or so after breakfast to get ready, but that turned out not to be the case.

Barbara and I stepped out into the Cedar Hill sunshine and there, a few yards away on this side of the street, its side-window shades down, the elephant in the living room, sat the meat wagon.

Barbara checked her watch. "They're prompt, I'll give them that much."

I looked from the wagon back to her. "You *knew* that it would be waiting for me?"

She said nothing; instead, she grabbed the envelopes from my hand and pointed to the one we'd written on: *People are listening.*

I nodded my understanding.

Barbara handed back the envelopes, then leaned in and gave me a kiss on the cheek. "You be careful, okay?"

"I'm expected to leave straight from *here?*"

"Yes."

"You might have mentioned that earlier."

"Why, you need to rearrange your social calendar?"

"Very funny."

"Sorry. I keep forgetting that you are a rock, you are an island."

"Do me a favor," I said, taking the cashier's check from the envelope and handing it to her. "Hang on to this until I get back. No way am I carrying that on me."

"I'll keep it safe." She slipped it into her purse. "Hey, when you get back, there's a junior partner in my office I'd like to introduce you to. I think you and her would hit it off."

"What self-respecting lawyer would want to date a janitor?"

She stared at me for a moment, then said: "I did. Once."

For a second, the ghost of Andy Leonard walked between us, then was gone.

"I'm sorry I made that 'social calendar' crack," she said.

"Forget it."

"No, no, I won't." She took hold of my hand. "I'm serious. You and I have lived here practically our entire lives, and in all that time I think I've seen you socially maybe a dozen times since high school, and even then it was by accident—bumping into you at a movie or a play or something. And you're always alone. I think Kimberly would really like you. Come on, what have you got to lose?"

"I don't know."

"Oh, *come on!* She's a redhead. You *know* you've got a thing for redheads. Dianne was a redhead."

"—a redhead who *divorced* me, thanks for bringing that up. Why do you even care? I don't mean that to sound defensive, I really don't, but why piss away any brain cells worrying about my social life or lack thereof?"

"That's a dumb question and I don't answer dumb questions. Doesn't matter, anyway, because I've already set it up. You're going out with her Saturday night."

"Oh, I am, am I?"

"Yes, you am." She squeezed my hand, then let go. "Drive Miss Driscoll home, come back safely, and take a chance on my matchmaking talents."

"Okay, fine." I gave her a quick hug and started walking toward the wagon, then turned back and said: "Thank you."

"You be careful, okay?"

"Will do."

It didn't occur to me until a few hours later that she had said something about being careful three times during that conversation.

The keys were in the wagon, as was a very expensive Montrachet mahogany coffin containing Miss Driscoll's body. A note from Dobbs was taped to the steering wheel: *Yes, she's in there, but feel free to check in case you want to see what the inside of an $8,000 coffin looks like.*

I decided to take his word for it.

I wondered if Dobbs had driven the wagon here, or if it had been one of the bulky shadows from last night, maybe one of their minions…or maybe the damn thing just materialized in the parking space.

You have no idea what you've gotten yourself into.

This had gone way past weird.

People are listening.

Whoever was orchestrating all of this seemed to be two steps ahead of everyone else. A brighter man would have had the good sense to be paranoid. A brighter man would have realized that Barb had told him three times to be careful. A brighter man would have suspected there was *something else* she hadn't told him. A brighter man would have known in the bottom of his gut that he was right smack in the middle of something really truly seriously goddamn *scary.*

Me, I took it as far as "weird" and left it at that.

I started the meat wagon and turned on the radio. Our local radio station was just finishing up its morning news update.

"…died this morning at Riverside Methodist Hospital in Columbus, bringing the total number of deaths from Sunday night's I-71 multi-car collision to seven."

That little tidbit of information both registered and didn't, as is the case with most things that come my way before noon. I scanned around until I found some music, then hit the road.

I have since come to the conclusion that my sole purpose in life is to serve as a warning to others.

6

I don't like maps. All the lines give me a headache, and half the time I'm so busy trying to interpret the miniscule printing I either miss the exit I'm looking for or almost drive into a guardrail—or sometimes even another car whose driver was so busy trying to read *his* map that he didn't see me coming.

Give me landmarks and I'm hell on wheels; give me a map and I turn into Forrest Gump in *Death Race 2000*.

Can you tell that driving is *not* my favorite thing in the world? Oh, with short distances I'm okay, but the fabled American Road Trip? Inwardly, I shriek in horror. Aside from the monotony, it gives you too long to think about things, and eventually your mind starts either sorting through useless trivia or dusting off memories best left in cold storage. Or, at least, mine does.

I'm good for about four or five hours cooped up inside a car, and then I need open space, food, and a bathroom—and that's the *best case* scenario, when I'm traveling with other people who can share the drive and conversation. (The last actual road trip I'd taken with another person was during the summer after high school graduation, when a bunch of us drove to Cleveland to see an Emerson, Lake & Palmer concert as our big pre-college blowout.)

Now imagine driving alone for well over a thousand miles with a corpse as your only companion. A Hope & Crosby *On The Road* movie this was not.

I'd been traveling for almost 14 hours and it was getting seriously dark. I was tired, I was upset, I was hungry, the coffin and its passenger were creeping me out to the *nth* degree, I needed to stretch my cramping legs, I'd missed the rest-stop entrance a few miles back (I was busy trying to make out the TripTik printing under the dim glow of the dome light), my bladder was grumpy, and I was pretty sure that I'd gotten onto the wrong stretch of highway at the interchange, so I decided, *fuck it*, I was going to take the next exit and find an all-night gas station and ask for directions.

That's right—*ask* for directions: I am not one these guys who feels genetically obligated to never admit that he's lost. If I'm going somewhere I just want to *get* there, preferably not *too far* behind schedule, in one piece and with my sanity intact; if that means I have to endure some twenty-something kid behind the counter of a Sip & Piss laughing at me under his breath as he shows me the best way to get back to where I need to be, well…there are worse humiliations that can be suffered, even if I sometimes *do* feel like belting that kid one upside the head. (And I *swear* it seems like it's always the same kid behind the counter, regardless of where you stop; personally, I think they're being manufactured in some top-secret government facility dedicated to creating as many aggravations as possible for American drivers so we don't notice that the gas prices always start to go up on Wednesday night, right about rush hour.)

According to my TripTik, the next exit—happy-happy-joy-joy—was twenty miles farther down the highway. If I was right and it turned out I should've taken the I-70 *West* ramp, then I was almost

25 miles away from where I should have taken the exit, which meant by the time I got back to where I needed to be I'd be about 50 miles in the hole.

I turned up the radio, which was tuned to a "classic rock" station, and was just in time to hear the DJ introduce The Who's "Baba O'Riley" with the words: "Can you believe this song is older than I am?"

I wanted to reach through the radio waves and strangle the little fucker.

I don't think of myself as being ancient (I'm only 44), but it still blows my mind that there are people out there who don't remember when "Baba O'Riley", "Won't Get Fooled Again", Zeppelin's "Stairway To Heaven", and even Deep Purple's "Smoke On The Water" were brand-new. Hell, half the DJs working these "classic rock" stations probably have no idea that "Smoke On The Water" *tanked* in the U.S. when it was released as a single from the *Machine Head* album; it was only when it was released as a single from *Made In Japan* that it became the monster smash—not to mention the first riff every kid learns to play once they get a guitar—we all know and pretend to loathe.

Told you my mind starts sorting through useless trivia if I spend too much time on the road, so don't start bitching about how this has nothing to do with anything.

I cranked up the volume and pressed down on the accelerator—almost anything from *Who's Next* turns me into a speed king—and before Roger Daltrey was finished roaring about the teenage wasteland, the exit was in sight.

Or, rather, *an* exit.

I checked the odometer and saw that it had been just under five miles; there wasn't supposed to be an exit for a while yet.

You know those moments in life that, when you talk about them later, you always preface with something like, "I should have known *because*..."? Well, there's no "because" here; yeah, what happened a few moments later was odd, no question, and I wish to hell I could say that I knew or sensed that something in the world was about to wander off the highway permanently, but the truth is there was nothing that set off any serious alarms. By now, I was so tired and cramped and sore and hungry and all the rest of it that I didn't *care* about the shadows that had broken into my apartment, or Miss Driscoll's morbid hobby, or the two thousand dollars, or my date with redheaded Kimberly—*nothing*.

On the TripTik map or not, that next exit was mine. If I'd turned down the radio and listened carefully, I bet I could have heard my bladder cheering.

That said, I can tell you now that if I had decided to wait for the following (and TripTik-*acknowledged*) exit farther down, all of this *still* would have happened—hell, I could have taken any exit from this point on and it wouldn't have changed anything.

The sign said, simply: **EXIT.** Nothing more; no town name, no number, no white arrow pointing in the correct direction. All of this both registered with me and didn't (like the total number of deaths from the I-71 accident); I saw it, knew something about it was odd, but just didn't care. I wanted to feel solid ground and not pedals under my feet for a few minutes.

As soon as I merged onto the ramp the light above the **EXIT** sign blinked twice, made a sputter-buzz kind of noise, then went out completely.

I wasn't prepared for how damned *black* it became after that. Nowhere on either side of me was there another light, so all I had to see by were the meat wagon's headlights. I clicked over to the brights and slowed down, just in case some possum, squirrel, dog, or deer decided to make a break for it and test my reflexes.

The first roadside memorial (a cross made of plastic flowers, sporting several ribbons) barely registered with me when it faded into the glow of the headlights. I drove on. The cross glided past. One of the ribbons snapped backwards and flapped in the breeze as if waving good-bye.

I thought of the miniature monuments Miss Driscoll had erected around her tracks.

Maybe it's just me, but I find something creepy about these monuments (be they HO-scale or life-size). I understand that those left behind have to do whatever it takes to deal with their grief, but if it were me and someone I'd loved had died in a wreck (probably in bloody pieces and great pain) the *last* goddamned place I'd want to erect a monument to their memory was the spot where their final agonized breath had been drawn and expelled. And since the maintenance of these things is the responsibility of those who erect them, that means you have to make an at-least quarterly pilgrimage to the place—assuming that you don't have to drive past it every day on your way to or from work. How can you pay suitable respect to someone's memory when you've got semis and SUVs and busloads of screaming kids roaring by every few seconds? Cemeteries may not be the cheeriest places to visit, but at least it *makes sense* to mourn there. Grieving by the side of the road in front of a monument no one but you gives a shit about just strikes me as distasteful…but then, I've never had to confront that particular kind of grief, so it's easy for me to pass judgment: Dianne—my ex-wife—always pointed that out to me—that it was easy for me to be judgmental about these memorials; she found them to be deeply moving.

Dianne never brought up my shortcomings to try and make me feel small; she did it because they, in her words: "…keep the best of you hidden from me and everyone else. You're not the cynic you want everyone to think you are." I never saw it that way, nope; as far as I was concerned, it was her way of proving to me once again that my moral compass was fucked up and wouldn't I be the best person if I saw the world *just like her*.

Yes, I was an asshole. It's taken all these years of being without her for that to finally sink in.

I looked in the rear-view mirror, saw the lone waving ribbon from the shrine, and felt a brief sting of regret—but for what, I wasn't sure.

"Baba O'Riley" segued into Grand Funk's "I'm Your Captain", and I turned up the volume, forcing myself to not think about the way Dianne detested this song.

The next shrine popped up as suddenly as a slice of bread from a toaster. This one was of the heart-shaped variety, but that isn't what startled me.

It was the sight of the face in the center.

It blinked at me.

And then smiled.

A sharp movement on the right of the shrine flashed against the windshield and I hit the brakes, thinking that some animal was about to make a mad dash for safety across the road, but instead of a raccoon or cat, what emerged from the side of the shrine was a hand, then a wrist, and then the face in the middle glided upward, leaving a blank space in the center—

—and the girl who was setting up the shrine waved at me.

I let out a breath I didn't realize I'd been holding and waved back at her, easing off the brake but not yet speeding up again.

Pushing back some of her long strawberry-blonde hair from her face, she looked at me, then at the shrine, and then shrugged, her smile looking more and more like that of a child who'd been caught doing something they shouldn't have been. Her clothing was dark—way too dark to be safe at this time of night, in this location.

Checking the dashboard clock, I saw that it was almost two in the morning, and there was no other car in sight. Had she walked here from whatever town lay at the end of the ramp? Why do this in the middle of the night when there was the chance someone might not see you until it was too late? And what the hell was I doing, sitting here wondering about this when I needed to be moving?

That's when it hit me that she wasn't trying to *erect* the shrine, she was trying to take it down, and I'd surprised her. This was probably some kind of sorority prank—she couldn't have been more than nineteen—and the look on her face told me that she was embarrassed but not necessarily sorry.

I looked at her, then the shrine, shook my head in disgust, and drove away.

She came out into the middle of the road and stood watching until I rounded the curve that emptied out into the town proper. I half expected her to give me the finger—after all, I'd been the one who had the *nerve* to interrupt her little practical joke—but she only stood there, arms at her sides, staring at my tail-lights.

Something about her shape seemed off to me, but I couldn't pin it down, and then decided I didn't care.

The second after I crested a small hill and she disappeared from view, I saw the stack of memorial wreaths, crosses, and hearts. They were piled up to the side at the traffic light like discarded bags of trash, plastic lace cracking, ribbons waving in the air, and countless photographed faces staring up through the open spaces in the center.

There must have been two dozen of the things piled there. I sat staring at them for several moments before turning to look out the rear window. Jesus, had she taken *all* of these? How far had she been walking, anyway? There was no way all of these had been taken from the small stretch of road along the exit, unless this particular exit was one of the deadliest in existence, which I doubted.

I looked back at the dead pile—that's how I suddenly thought of it, and had *no* idea where the hell the phrase had come from—then decided, *screw the light*, made my turn, and headed toward the service station about a quarter-mile down the street. I didn't know what she was up to and I didn't want to know. I'd gas up, take a piss (well, *leave* one, actually), get my directions, and mind my own business the rest of the way to Miss Driscoll's home town.

Still, it angered me to think that, sitting in some sorority house somewhere, a bunch of smug sisters were giggling over this prank and not giving one thought to the additional grief it would bring to those whose heartbreak had compelled them to mark the place of their loved one's death.

And *that* thought struck me as funny: *Hey, Dianne, here's a question: What is the sound made by a moral compass shifting?*

I exhaled, shook my head, and turned down the radio as I pulled into the service station.

It was surprisingly modern for what appeared at first glance to be a very small town; automated pay-here pumps, a diesel docking area, an attached car wash, and one of those seemingly hermetically-sealed booths where the "attendant" sat behind inch-thick glass and you made purchases after midnight through a series of metal drawers.

I swiped my credit card (I was saving the cash for emergencies), waited for the pump to authorize my purchase, and looked over to see the attendant staring right at me and talking into the phone. He looked nervous, maybe even a little scared, and for a crazy moment I thought, *He's calling the cops.*

(Help, dear God, help me—I've got an actual customer! What'll I do? I'm doomed! Doomed, I tell you!)

Then it occurred to me: I was driving a meat wagon, clearly marked **CORONER.** That'd freak out anyone at this time of night.

The authorization came through and I filled the tank, got my receipt, and decided to give the windshield a quick wash. I was wiping away the last of the cleaner when I asked myself: What would Dianne do if she were here?

Dianne could never, *never* see a wrong without at least *trying* to take some kind of action, even if all that action amounted to was pointing out to someone that the wrong was being committed. I made her believe that this annoyed the hell out of me, which in truth it did—not because it was another way of her proving how moral she was, but because I admired the courage it took to always do it, and in my admiration found that same conviction to be sadly lacking in myself, which irritated me, so more often than not I took it out on her in a series of little cruelties that ran the gamut from deliberately ignoring her to going out of my way to be a pain in the ass. I was a real prince of a hubby, me.

So the question: *What would Dianne do?*

She'd tell someone, that's what.

I looked at the kid in the booth, then back at my car, then at my feet. Staring at my feet has been the source of many an epiphany over the years.

I was surprised to discover that I was genuinely pissed at what that girl was doing back there.

Next thing I know, I'm standing at the booth and waiting for the kid to look up from the issue of *Guitar Player* that he's reading. Steve Morse was on the cover. I like Steve Morse's music a lot. Perhaps I could use that as an ice-breaker if the little shit ever acknowledged my existence.

Finally I cleared my throat, and without looking up from the page he was reading, the kid reached out and pressed on the intercom button: "Yeah?"

"There's a girl about a mile back who's vandalizing some roadside memorials."

"You don't say?" He looked at me with the kind of unctuous, smarmy smirk that doesn't try to mask the wearer's amused apathy, and instantly makes you want to step on their face and grind your heel.

Keeping a civil tongue, I quickly explained to him what I'd seen, and where, and finished by suggesting that he call the police or sheriff.

That smirk still on his face, he nodded, flipped to a new page in the magazine, and said: "Anything else I can do for you?"

I tried, Dianne; give me that much. I tried.

"Yes," I said. "Where are your restrooms?"

This got an audible sigh. He closed the magazine, stood up (which seemed to be a source of great physical strain), walked over to a cabinet on the wall, opened the door, and removed a key that was attached to a chain that was soldered to a piece of metal half the length of my forearm. Returning to his stool (I saw now that one of his legs was encased in a metal brace of some kind), he valiantly struggled back into position, tossed the key into a drawer, then shoved it out to me.

Removing the works from the drawer, I waited for him to say something. When he didn't, I used the end of the key to tap on the glass. Hearing it, he paused in his reading, sighed even more loudly than before, and (still not looking up at me) said: "*Yes?*"

I couldn't help but wonder how long he'd last in this job if it actually required him to step outside and *work* for his paycheck, metal leg brace or no. "This does me no good unless you tell me where the restrooms are."

He pointed to his left. That's all the more I was going to get from him as far as directions went; past left, I was on my own.

I nodded, turned away, muttered, "If I don't return, let it be on your conscience," and made my way around the left side of the building.

The restrooms, as it turned out, were at the *back* of the building, which meant I had to go left, walk the length of the place, then turn right. Night vision goggles would have helped me locate the door quicker, since the back of the place—despite the glaring lights from the pump islands—was mostly in shadow, but I'm pleased to say that I didn't have to add a stop at an all-night department store for a new pair of pants to my travels.

I found the restroom, unlocked the door, and made it inside.

I have been in kitchens in peoples' homes that weren't as clean as this restroom. It not only smelled brand-new, it *looked* brand-new: the floor tile was shiny, the faucets sparkled, the mirrors were streak-free, someone had decorated the *wood-paneled* walls with framed photographs and old movie posters, there was none of that moist, old-urinal-cake stink that usually permeates service station bathrooms (the urinals and toilets looked as if they'd never been used), and there was no trash in the receptacles—not a paper towel, wad of chewing gum, empty soda can, nothing.

I almost felt like I was defiling the place when I finally stepped up to the urinal, but an aching bladder will diminish the sanctity of even the Sistine Chapel; yes, you may quote me on that.

Standing there, I looked around at the movie posters and photographs. I was expecting stuff like *Gone with the Wind* and pictures of New York at night—your standard, safe, pleasant, nothing-to-offend-anyone type of public restroom *milieu,* but instead what I got were posters for *Two-Lane Blacktop*, *Vanishing Point*, *Dirty Mary and Crazy Larry, The Driver,* and (the one that made me laugh out loud) *Death Race 2000*. Whoever decorated in here had a thing for racing and car-chase movies.

The photographs were of people standing beside heavily tricked-out or racing cars; a couple looked to have been taken in the winner's circle at NASCAR or Formula One races (I don't know the difference between the two, it's all just roaring engines and squealing tires to me).

Then I turned my attention back to the business at hand and caught a glimpse of the framed photograph hanging over my urinal.

Have you ever heard someone say, *It scared the piss out of me*? Well, if there's an expression for the opposite bladder-related physical reaction to being frightened, it pretty much describes what happened when I saw that photograph, because everything south of my personal Mason-Dixon line came to sudden, dribbling halt; it felt like my bladder would have slammed everything into reverse had it been capable.

I was looking at a very striking woman surrounded by dozens of children, all of them smiling the type of forced, could-you-*hurry*-up-and-take-the-picture-*puh-leeeeze* smile that we've all plastered on our faces at one time or another as suited the occasion.

This wasn't a copy of the picture from Miss Driscoll's foyer—it was the *same photograph*, in the same frame, with the same crack in the glass running down the center of her face.

Of all the thoughts that could have gone through my mind, these are the three things that occurred to me at that moment: 1) the hulking shadows in my apartment had not used any doors or windows to break in or to leave; 2) another shadow had closed the door to Miss Driscoll's apartment *from the inside* after Dobbs had made certain it locked behind us; and, 3) if these shadows could just pop in and out when- and wherever they wanted, who was to say they couldn't bring something along…like, say, this picture?

Take a good look: this is me, not realizing I'm screwed.

This is me, not realizing I'm screwed while still holding my dick in my hand. And dribbling piss onto my shoes.

A moment of great personal dignity that I felt compelled to share. I feel it's brought us closer.

Backing away from the urinal, zipping up, and wanting to look over my shoulder to see if someone or something were standing behind me, I found I couldn't take my eyes off that photograph. There were probably, oh, at least one or one-and-a-half very good, logical, *reasonable* scenarios to explain how this picture had followed me to this place, but at that moment I couldn't think of any that didn't involve bulky shadows. And even if I could have, all of them would have shared the same ending, anyway; me getting the hell out of Dodge right now.

Except—as I was about to find out—Dodge had other plans.

7

Coming around the side of the building, I blinked against the strobe-light glow cast by the whirling visibar lights atop the Sheriff's Department vehicle parked at an angle in front of the meat wagon. It appeared that I wasn't going anywhere for the moment.

Plastering what I hoped was a genuinely innocent smile on my face, I started toward the nearest uniform and said, "Is there a prob—"

He held up his hand—*Please be quiet*—as he spoke into the radio microphone. "He just came out of the bathroom. Call Impound and let 'em know."

Impound? I looked around. What the hell did he think—

—*You have no idea what you've gotten yourself into*—

—the meat wagon now had a passenger, as well as some additional cargo.

Young Miss Memorial sat in the passenger seat. Behind her, crammed in none-too-carefully, were the contents of the Dead

Pile; wreathes, crosses, and several hearts, all of them now sans photographs, all of them having scattered ribbons and plastic flowers around the interior as well as over Miss Driscoll's oh-so expensive coffin.

I couldn't have been in the restroom for more than three minutes, yet somehow in that time Young Miss Memorial had not only managed to cover a good two-and-half miles of road on foot, but did so while carrying all of her evening's roadside pickings. I doubted that the things were all that heavy individually *or* cumulatively, but their collective bulk was enough to tell me no way could she have done this on her own.

So who'd helped her?

The sheriff finished talking to whomever he'd radioed, then signaled to his deputy, who promptly came up behind me and shoved the business end of a revolver into my back. Always priding myself on taking a subtle hint when one is offered, I slowly raised my hands.

"We're not going to have any problems, are we?" said the sheriff, looking down at his feet.

Momentarily unable to summon a witty retort, I just shook my head.

"You have some paperwork to show me?"

When I neither spoke nor nodded, the deputy pressed his gun farther into my back.

"My inside coat pocket," I managed to get out.

The sheriff reached in and removed the envelope, took out the FRTP, read it over, then said, "Okay, then. Let's go."

"Go where?"

He nodded toward the meat wagon. “You’re under arrest for vandalism, theft of city property, and contributing to the delinquency of a minor.”

Young Miss Memorial smiled at us, held up an open can of beer, then gave the gas station attendant a little wave.

“This is bullshit,” I said.

The sheriff took a step closer to me. “Oh?”

“I didn’t take those goddamn things and you know it. I’d tell you to ask him—” I nodded toward the attendant, “—but something tells me his memory might be a little fuzzy.”

The sheriff looked over at the attendant. For a moment I thought he was actually going to ask the guy, then just as quickly realized what I should have known all along: they were all in on it. No, Young Miss Memorial couldn’t have moved the Dead Pile so quickly on her own, but with a squad car and a couple of guys to help her—no sweat.

At least now I knew who the attendant had been calling when I first pulled in. What I didn’t know was *why*.

Summoning all the nerve I had under the circumstances, I said, “I’m not going anywhere.”

This got a huge laugh out of the sheriff as he pushed back his hat, giving me my first clear view of his face.

He was a *kid*. Nineteen, twenty years old, tops.

“Here’s the thing,” he said, tucking the FRTP back into my pocket. “It’s after two o’clock in the morning. You’re not where you expected to be—you’re where you’re *supposed* to be, sure, but my guess is you were figuring on—what?—at least a few more hours of road time. Doesn’t matter.” He got right up in my face then. “It’s the middle of the night. No one, and I mean *no one*, including you, knows where you are right now. *We've* got guns. You're in possession of vandalized and stolen property. And there's an underage girl in your front seat with an open container of alcohol. So you don't get to say where you will or will not go or what you will or will not do."

I wondered how many Raymond Chandler novels he'd had to read in order to teach himself to talk that way, but figured this wouldn't be a good time to ask, so instead I opted for, "I want to talk to someone in authority whose age is higher than my shirt size, if that's all right with you."

"Fair enough. If you'll shut the hell up and get into the back seat of my vehicle, I'll take you to that person."

I nodded toward the meat wagon. "What about—?"

The sheriff held out his hand. "The keys."

I gave them to him. "Anything happens to that vehicle or the body, and I'm gonna be in a lot of trouble."

He smiled. "Nothing's going to happen. These streets are safe. Hell, a person couldn't have an accident if they *tried*." He walked over and handed the keys to Young Miss Memorial.

"Does Daddy Bliss know that Road Mama's come home?" she asked him.

The sheriff nodded. "He knows. Everyone knows by now." He patted the top of the wagon, and then smiled. "I like how that sounds, 'Road Mama's come home.'"

Young Miss Memorial smiled back at him. "Me, too."

Road Mama and Daddy Bliss. Sounded like the name of some *faux* country & western ballad from 1970's pop radio, a rip-snortin', high-ballin', pedal-to-the-metal toe-tapper you'd hear sandwiched between C.W. McCall's "Convoy" and Jerry Reed's theme from

Smoky and the Bandit. If I hadn't been so angry and scared (mostly scared), I might have laughed at the thought.

The sheriff leaned down to whisper something in Young Miss Memorial's ear. The back of his jacket pulled tight, and for a moment I thought, *he's got five spines*, because that's how it looked. It was only as he stood back up and I heard a pronounced metallic scrape and the rustle of straining Velcro that I realized he was wearing some kind of complicated back brace.

Without thinking, I asked, "Does that hurt?"

"I beg your pardon?"

I gestured toward him. "That brace you're wearing. Does it hurt?"

He stared at me for a few seconds, blinked, then replied, "Sometimes. What's it to you?'

I shrugged. "I'm just wondering why you weren't assigned desk duty until you healed up."

"Because, Mother Theresa, I'm not *going* to heal up."

"I meant no offense."

"Nobody ever does." He opened the back door of his cruiser. "Any more questions, or can we get on with this?"

I ducked down my head and climbed in behind the shotgun seat, surprised to see no wire-mesh divider separating the back seat from the front.

The deputy who'd been holding the gun in my back slid in on the other side of me, closed the door, and removed his hat. He looked, if anything, even younger than the sheriff. Round face, bright grey eyes, flushed cheeks…sixteen, at most. Plus he was smaller than the sheriff, so his uniform was pulled in and tucked tightly so it wouldn't hang too loosely. He might as well have been a big-for-his age child playing Policeman. If it weren't for the metal plate covering the right side of his skull, I might have even *believed* he was a little kid.

If he noticed the way I stared at him, he gave no indication.

The plate itself was a dull shade of silver, tinged at the edges with a crusty red substance where the jagged flesh of his grayish, moist-looking scalp fused with the metal. There were six screws in all, one at each corner of the plate, with one extra on the upper and lower sides. None of them matched. Some were small and thin, others were thick, and one looked, I swear, like a cement screw. Most were flush, but two rose slightly above the surface.

He finally noticed that I was staring, and so moved to brush some of his hair back in a futile effort to cover at least a portion of the plate. All he succeeded in doing was showing me that part of his scalp had been peeled completely away near the base of the plate, offering me a glimpse of skull.

"What happened to you?" I asked.

He shrugged. "This looks a lot better than it did. Shoulda seen it before I got fixed up."

The sheriff climbed into the driver's seat, closing his door with more force than was needed. "What have I told you about flashing that thing at people? *Put your hat back on, Dash*."

"You took yours off just now."

"That's because I'm driving and need an unobstructed view. If you were driving, then you could take *yours* off. But you're not driving, Dash. *You'r*e in the back seat scaring the living shit out of our prisoner for no good reason other than you can. Now put your hat back on, or I'm gonna tell everyone it's okay to start calling you 'Chop-Top' again."

"You wouldn't do that."

The sheriff turned around to face him. "No, I probably wouldn't, but that should give you some idea of how much this bothers me. You know that Daddy Bliss had them make that hat especially for you. It's got that steel band around the inside and everything."

Deputy Dash blinked. "I know. Gets pretty hot with it on. And heavy."

The sheriff gave me a quick look—*Kids, what're you gonna do?*—and then sighed. "If you wear the hat, Dash, then you won't get so many headaches, and you won't hear so many voices."

Deputy Dash leaned over toward me. "This plate picks up radio waves sometimes."

"And sometimes," said the sheriff, "it *interferes* with them. Like when I need to call in." He held up the microphone. "So will you please put it back on?"

"See there?" said Deputy Dash. "All you had to do was say 'please'." He donned his hat once again. "Just ask me nice, that's all. Don't order me like you're my boss or something."

The sheriff hung down his head. "Dash, I *am* your boss."

"You know what I mean."

We pulled out of the gas station, the meat wagon following close behind.

I stared at Deputy Dash. "How come you're called Dash?"

He pointed to the metal plate. "'Cause that's where my head hit."

I nodded as if that cleared up everything. "Oh. You get FM with that?"

He grinned. "You're funny. We don't get many funny ones."

He was still holding his gun on me.

"Could you maybe point that toward the floor?" I asked. "If we hit a bump or something, it might go off."

"It don't work."

"What?"

"His gun isn't loaded," said the sheriff. Glancing into his rearview mirror, his gaze momentarily met mine. "I mean, *look at him*. Don't misunderstand, he's my kid brother and I love him, but seriously—would *you* feel safe knowing he was in possession of live ammunition?"

Deputy Dash held up his weapon. "Sure is big, though. That usually does the trick."

"And what if it doesn't?" I asked.

"Then I use my gun," said the sheriff. "*My* gun is loaded."

Deputy Dash puffed up a bit as he said, "But it ain't nearly as big."

"You can put your gun away now, Dash."

"Nah."

"What was that?"

Deputy Dash looked up at his brother. "If I have to put my gun away, then the hat comes off. Since I have to keep my hat on, the gun stays out."

"Why can't you wear your hat *and* put your gun away?" asked the sheriff.

"On account I need to have something in my hands to play with or I get jumpy, and if I can't have either my hat or my gun, that just leaves my dick, and the last time I played with my dick in the car, you throwed a hissy fit."

"That's because you never clean up after yourself!"

"I do so!"

The sheriff pounded his fist against the door. "You wipe up the *seat*, sure, but you never clean the dashboard *or* the steering wheel! You got any idea how it feels to start my day by coming out to the cruiser and then grabbing the wheel to find your day-old spooge all over it?"

Dash shrugged. "Never bothered me."

"That's because it's *your spooge! Of course* it's not gonna bother you, just like my farts don't bother *me*. In fact, I think my farts smell *just fine!*"

"Then how come you keep a can of air freshener in the glove compartment?"

"Because you're always complaining about how my farts stink up the car."

"Yeah, but whenever you use that air freshener, all it does it make it smell like someone squeezed out a load of Cleveland Steamers in a rose garden."

I cleared my throat. "This sounds like a private family matter to me. If you want to pull over and let me out, I'd be glad to—"

The sheriff let go of the steering wheel and spun around, his arm shooting straight out, holding his gun less than an inch from my face.

"Shut the hell up!" he screamed at me, cocking the hammer. "You've already caused enough trouble, *Driver*. You think this is funny? You getting a chuckle out of listening to me argue with my brain-damaged little brother? It's not his fault he's the way he is."

"Thank you," said Dash.

"You're welcome." He looked back at me. "You keep your comments and your questions to yourself until I say otherwise. One more word out of you, Driver—*one more fucking word*—and I will shoot you in the kneecap. Do you understand me?"

I nodded.

"We all appreciate that you brought Road Mama back home, but if someone told you that your job ended once she was delivered, well…that's probably what they were told, but it's not true. Ah-ah—*not. One. Word.*"

I mimed zipping closed my mouth.

"He's funny," said Dash. "We don't get many funny ones."

"You said that already."

"Felt like saying it again."

I went cold all over. I could feel the blood draining from my face. Yeah, the gun and the look in the sheriff's eyes were scary enough—there was no doubt in my mind that he'd shoot me in the kneecap if I gave him the excuse—but even those seemed minor compared to what I'd just realized.

The car was driving itself.

Ever since the sheriff had spun around in his seat, the car had continued to maneuver along the street just as smoothly and evenly as you please. It even decelerated and signaled when cornering.

The sheriff noticed I wasn't staring at him or his gun. Looking over his shoulder, he hissed, *"Shit!"* and then turned back around, holstering his weapon and gripping the spooge-free wheel once again. "I'm sorry. You weren't supposed to see that yet."

"Oops," said Dash, then giggled.

I opened my mouth to ask, "See *what* yet?" but my kneecaps reminded me that, ahem, silence was golden.

The sheriff grabbed up the microphone again. "Nova, darlin', you there?"

"Of *course* I am, where else would I be?"

"I think I just screwed up."

"Oh, dear. What have you gone and done?"

He told her. There were several moments of silence, and then Nova said, "Well, now, that doesn't sound all *that* bad. You just hold on and I'll get right back to you."

"Will do."

He glanced in the rearview mirror at me. "May be that we'll have a change of plans."

I mimed unzipping my mouth.

"I think he wants to ask you something," said Dash.

"He can talk."

"You *know* I didn't take those memorials, right?"

"Yeah, I know."

"And I sure as hell didn't give that girl a ride *or* a beer. Especially not *light* beer."

"There a point you're getting to?"

"Yeah—why all the bullshit and brouhaha?"

"Needed to make sure you'd come along peacefully."

"Why not just *ask* me?"

"Wasn't sure you'd say yes."

"And if I hadn't?"

"Then we'd've had to resort to the bullshit and brouhaha, anyway. Just seemed easier to go with the sure thing."

I looked at Dash, who offered a shrug that said, *Older brothers, what're you gonna do?*

I leaned forward against the front seat. "You said something about a 'change' of plans? Would you mind telling me what the *original* plan was supposed to be? For that matter, what the hell was that girl *doing* back there, gathering up all those memorials? And how is it that this goddamn cruiser can drive itself? Now that I think of it, *where am I*, exactly? I'm not supposed to be anywhere *near* my destination. And what is it with everyone and—"

"You know what?" said the sheriff. "I changed my mind. Shut up or I'll shoot you."

"No, you won't."

He turned around and shot me.

There was a lot of confusion right after that, what with the too-bright muzzle-flash, the gargantuan noise made by the shot in the enclosed space, and me screaming like a *castrato* with flaming hemorrhoids. Grabbing my happy sacs—that's where he'd aimed—I knew *something* had happened down there because I could smell the gunshot and feel the heat between my legs and God Almighty there was something wet under my hands but I was too busy screeching and waiting for the pain to register, then I caught a peripheral glimpse of Deputy Dash laughing his ass off and realized that the sheriff hadn't shot *me*, he'd shot the portion of the seat between my legs, and what I was feeling beneath my hand wasn't blood gushing out of the hole where my nuts had previously resided but plain old-fashioned urine.

"Good shot!" shouted Dash.

"Like hell!" yelled the sheriff. "I *missed*."

"*I'm sorry!*" I screamed at him, my voice breaking on the second word. "Jesus Christ, I'm sorry! I didn't…I didn't mean anything."

"Do you believe that I *will* shoot you?"

"Yes!"

"All right then." He turned back, holstered his weapon, and took hold of the wheel once more.

I have no idea how long I cowered in the back seat with my knees pulled up against my chest, shaking and trying not to cry. I *hate* showing weakness in front of others. It gives them the upper hand and diminishes me in my own eyes.

Eventually, Dash leaned over and put his hand on my shoulder. I jumped at his touch and slammed the top of my head against the roof.

"Sorry," he said. "I shouldn't have laughed."

All I could do was nod my head, and even *that* hurt like hell.

"We can get you some clean pants and underwear," said Dash.

"…would be nice…" I heard myself whisper.

Then the radio crackled and the dispatcher's voice chimed in. "You still there, Hummer?"

He grabbed the microphone. "Where else would I be?"

"That's my line, Sheriff."

"Sue me."

"*Touchy* tonight, aren't we?"

"Did you talk with Daddy Bliss?"

"No, I just missed the sound of your voice—*of course* I talked with him."

"*And…?*"

"And Daddy says, no worries. He wanted Driver to have the grand tour, anyway."

Hummer stared out at the road, saying nothing for a few seconds, looking confused.

I leaned toward Dash. "Is that a nickname, 'Hummer'?"

"Nope."

Sheriff Hummer was still speaking to the dispatcher. "When's the tour supposed to start?"

"As soon as possible."

"Can we at least get him a change of clothes first?"

"A change of clothes?" said Nova. "What did you—never mind. Sure thing. He can look through the wardrobe when he gets here."

"Call our ETA five minutes. Ciera's right behind us with Road Mama."

"You want me to call Stick and tell him to hit the lights?"

Hummer glanced in the rearview mirror toward me, then said, "Might as well."

"Oh, you're gonna like this," said Dash. "Ain't everyone who gets to see Levegh Lane."

"Why's that?"

Deputy Dash shrugged. "We don't get many visitors."

"So this is a big deal, huh?"

"Yep."

"Why…why do you call it that? Is there some significance to the name? Is that Daddy Bliss's real name or something?"

Hummer answered this one: "It's named after Pierre Levegh, a race car driver. Drove a Mercedes at Le Mans in 1955. In the third hour of the race, this Jaguar driver named Mike Hawthorn got a signal from his pit crew to stop for gas. He slowed down, but there was this Austin-Healey right on his ass, and it had to swerve to avoid him. A little ways behind, Levegh raised his hand to signal another car to slow the hell down. Levegh was going 150 miles per hour." Hummer shook his head. "He never had a chance.

"Levegh slammed into the Healey and his car took off like a rocket, crashed into the embankment beside the track, hurtled end over end, and then just disintegrated over the crowd. The hood decapitated a bunch of spectators. The engine and front axle cut through a bunch of people, splitting them in half. The car had a magnesium body, right, and that son-of-a-bitch burst into flames like a torch, burning dozens of others to death. The whole thing took maybe 12 seconds, but in that time 82 people were killed and 76 others were maimed."

I blinked. "And you *named a street* after him?"

"That's right. Levegh was a great man."

"A *great* man," said Dash.

Hummer nodded. "Only a truly heroic man could bring so many new members into Road Mama and Daddy Bliss's family in a few brief seconds."

Do I need to tell you exactly *how* anxious this little exchange made me? It finally sank in that I was trapped in a car with a couple of out-patients. If my luck held up, we'd soon be passing the Bates Motel.

I was so scared but I was also damned if I was going to show it; at least, no more than I already had.

"You might want to sit up," said Hummer. "Make sure you can get a good look out the window. You might not know it, but this a great honor, Daddy Bliss wanting you to see everything."

I heard a distant buzzing noise, like a massive electrical grid warming up. Even through the vibration of the tires against the streets I could feel the deep, powerful thrum that rose in power with the pitch of the grid.

"You might want to prepare yourself some," said Hummer. "This could be a bit of a shock."

That didn't even *begin* to cover it.

8

The street exploded with light, bright and blinding, bearing down like a curse from Heaven and forcing me to close my eyes and throw my arms up against my face.

After the stars stopped going supernova behind my lids, I slowly opened my eyes and saw that both sides of this cliff-lined street were being illuminated by rows upon rows of huge stadium lights that rose easily a hundred feet above the surface of the road. I wondered how they'd managed to install them at the tops of the cliffs, and then realized that these weren't cliffs at all.

They were cars.

Crushed, smashed, mangled, and twisted, stacked dozens atop dozens, held together by steel beams and girders that had been welded into place to form main spannings and supports, creating something like a life-sized shadowbox. The stacks

(*dead piles?*)

rose so high I almost couldn't see the tops of the damn things. Each car-cube was roughly the size of a large building, nine or ten stories high, separated from its neighbor by a space of maybe 30 feet. It was in those spaces where the stadium light towers were installed, and as we passed the first group and I looked through those spaces I saw that the car-cubes not only lined both sides of the street but extended backward for what seemed miles, a giant child's building block set, each one placed at a point equidistant from those beside, in front of, and behind it. It was like something out of an Escher painting.

"Where did all of these come from?" I asked.

"Everywhere," replied Dash. "They come from all over the place in the U.S."

"And sometimes Canada or Mexico," said Sheriff Hummer. "If someone drives here from Canada or Mexico, they're on our roads, so their ass is ours if something happens."

"'Ours'?" I said.

"Ours," replied Dash.

"Well, technically," said Hummer, "they belong to Road Mama and Daddy Bliss, but since the rest of us are family, we like to think of them as 'ours'. That answer your question?"

"Not really."

"Don't worry, things'll be explained to you."

Ciera came up alongside us in the meat wagon, waving and smiling before hitting the turn signal and taking a side road.

"She's using the shortcut," said Dash.

Hummer nodded his head. "I got eyes, little brother."

"Daddy Bliss told us we weren't supposed to take no shortcuts tonight."

"And Ciera will have to explain herself to him, so it's not our problem."

"But he won't do anything to her, he never does. It ain't *fair!* How come she gets to do whatever she wants and the rest of us gotta do as we're told?"

"Because Daddy Bliss favors Ciera, you know that. She was the last person he brought into the family himself."

Dash folded his arms across his chest and pressed his chin down, pouting. "Yeah, well, *still* it ain't fair."

"Not much is, little brother. Don't need to keep reminding ourselves."

We made a left, turning onto a stretch of road where the car-cubes were replaced by typical middle-class houses on a typical middle-class street. All the lights were on inside each house, and several people were standing on their front porches, watching us pass by.

"Gonna be a big night for everyone here, Driver," said Hummer. "A *big* night."

I swallowed, leaning forward. "Why are you called 'Hummer'?"

The sheriff looked into the rear-view mirror. "Because that's what I was driving when I got myself and my little brother killed. It was my fault, I was screwing around, pretending that the goddamn thing was a tank. I accidentally side-swiped a semi, lost control of the wheel, and went over the side of a bridge."

"I was pretty scared," said Dash. "I was all bent over and crying. That's how I busted open my head on the bottom of the dashboard."

"And I was the driver," replied the sheriff. "That's how it works."

I returned his stare in the rear-view mirror for a few moments more, then said, "Fuck you."

"What was that?" One of his hands snapped down to the butt of his gun.

"I said fuck you. I'm supposed to believe that you two are dead, is that it?"

"We ain't dead," said Dash.

"Just Repaired," said Hummer. He pronounced the second word with such awe and reverence I could almost see the capital 'R'.

I looked at the houses we were passing. The people on the porches all had something wrong with them; some used canes or crutches, some were in wheelchairs, others had arms missing or in slings, and a couple of them wore those square metal-cage get-ups that people who suffer severe neck injuries are saddled with using.

"What about them?" I asked, nodding toward the onlookers.

"Repaired," said Hummer. "Everyone who lives here has been Repaired or is in the process of being Repaired. Sometimes the Repairs aren't that big of a deal, like with Dash and Ciera and me. But some Repairs, they take a bit of work."

Dash looked at me and nodded his head.

"So this is, what? Zombie Town U.S.A.?"

Hummer glared at me. "I'd watch the sarcasm if I was you. And, no, there aren't any zombies here. Only the Repaired."

We turned off the street and hit a long patch that wound through a heavily industrialized section of town. Factories small and large lined both sides of the road for nearly three miles, and judging from the amount of noise and smoke pouring from each building, things were busy.

It was only as we were turning off onto another street that I caught a glimpse of any of the factory workers (which I think was Hummer's intention, seeing as how he was driving not only slowly but quite close to the curb). A large set of heavy iron doors were open, giving me a clear look into the foundry where one of the workers was emptying a vat of white-hot molten metal into an arc furnace. Despite the shimmering heat waves and sparks scattering as the liquid metal gushed down, I got a very clear look at the man.

His right arm had been replaced by a steel prosthesis whose components had been molded, bent, twisted, and press-punched into something that was meant to look organic and serve the same function as his missing arm. It had an elbow joint that bent easily enough and a semi-robotic hand with five finger-like appendages. The wires and conduits that snaked through the openings in the metal were in a configuration comparable to that of veins. The prosthesis moved stiffly, and every time the worker turned his back to us, the highly-polished sheet of silver chrome used to replace his shoulder blade caught the light and threw it back into my eyes. I was still blinking when the worker stopped what he was doing, rose straight up, and—like he'd known all along that he was being observed—turned to face me.

The left half of his face had been Repaired, as well. I saw the bright protruding taillight that had taken the place of his eye, the section of sheared metal that served as his jawbone, and what I swear looked like seat leather that now replaced the flesh of his cheek.

He lifted his robotic hand and waved.

"Believe me now," said Hummer, "or do you want us to get out so I can make a personal introduction?"

"Incredible" was all I could get out.

"No," said Dash, "just Repaired, that's all. Ain't no big thing, really."

Hummer laughed and sped up the cruiser.

I turned around in the seat, staring out the rear window, and saw the foundry worker walk out into the middle of the street and watch us drive away. Even after his body disappeared into shadow, I could still see the bright red light of his Repaired eye.

I was about to ask Hummer where they got the parts to Repair people, then thought of the car-cubes and knew the answer.

9

We pulled up in front of a large concrete building that contained few windows and began to park.

"If he's getting the tour," said Dash, "then shouldn't we take him in through the back?"

"Shit," said Hummer, backing out of the space, "you're right. Thanks for reminding me."

"You're welcome."

We drove around to the back where a single streetlight provided little illumination. We got out, and then entered the building through a heavy steel door.

The first thing that hit me was the smell of the place; it was a combination of that sweaty, metallic, smoky, machine-grease stench of the factory floor and the overly-antiseptic aroma of a hospital corridor. I'd never smelled anything like it in my life.

"You get used to the smell," said Hummer, clamping a hand on my elbow and leading me through a set of doors on the left. Dash made a beeline for a set of doors on the right—the vending machine area.

We entered a somewhat cramped but well-lit office filled with scuffed wooden desks and chairs that were easily 30 years out of date, the furniture made all the more anachronistic by the expensive state-of-the-art equipment setting on it: 25-inch flat screen LCD monitors on broken roll-top desks, iMacs being used by people sitting in slat-backed wooden chairs held together in places with duct tape, and a trio of huge 50-inch plasma televisions mounted on the walls displaying a slide-show series of maps, as well as images from what I assumed were security cameras; empty streets, empty corridors, empty parking lots.

"It's impolite to stare," said Hummer, pulling me toward a door marked **Holding Room** at the back of the office. Opening the door, he reached in and flipped on the light, then pushed me inside. "Bathroom's on the right, and there're snacks in the refrigerator." He pointed to a rolling metal rack filled with hanging clothes. "Nova's already had some stuff from the wardrobe put in here, so you can change out of those pissy clothes. Clean yourself up and get a bite to eat. You won't be in here for too long."

"Wait a second," I said as he began closing the door.

He paused. "*Yes?*"

I took a deep breath and summoned what little nerve I still had. "Aren't I entitled to one phone call?"

"You are."

"I'd like to make it, please."

Hummer grinned. "Who have you got to call, Driver?"

"That's my business."

"More like your daydream, from what I understand."

Glaring at him, I made a fist but did not raise it. "I demand my right to a phone call."

"You'll get your call, stop whining." He stared at me for a moment, his features softening a bit. "You're really *scared*, aren't you?"

"Yes."

Hummer looked over his shoulder, then stepped back into the holding room, pushing the door most of the way closed. "Listen to me, Driver. I don't know what you did to piss off the Highway People, but it must have been pretty goddamn serious for you to wind up here. The folks who come to this place, they don't *drive* in, and they sure as hell don't *leave*. *Nobody* just passes through here, the Highway People won't let them. But *you*, you're getting special treatment. I can't tell you whether or not you're gonna leave here alive because I don't get to make that call, but I *can* tell you that no one, the Highway People included, has any intention of harming you. Anything that might or might not happen to you will be your own doing, not ours."

I was still trying to get past *I can't tell you whether or not you're gonna leave here alive* when I heard myself asking, "Who are the Highway People?"

Hummer shrugged. "That's just what we call them. I don't know what their actual names are—hell, I don't even know if they *have* names. They've been around as long as there have been roads and cars. I guess they're—dunno—the gods of the road."

"Have you ever seen them?"

"Once. Right after the accident. They came for me and Dash." He was staring out at something only he could see. For the first time that night, he looked so much older than his years. "I remember," he said, "that the windows were rolled halfway down—it was a warm night, Dash had his open and so did I, so when we went over the bridge and hit the water below, these *swords* of water slashed through the interior. I guess that happened because when we hit, we made a mother of a splash, it happened so fast, and we were both panicking because the interior was filling up and we were trying to get our seatbelts undone. Dash's arms were flailing all over the place and he kept looking in the back seat for something, and I remember that those first swords of water felt like they'd actually *gone in*, y'know? Straight through flesh and into the bone. Even though everything was happening very fast and I *knew* it was happening very fast, in my eyes it was all in slow motion. Getting my seat belt off and then trying to help Dash with his, and that's when I saw that he was already dead. His arms weren't flailing, they were just floating, and the reason he was looking in the back seat was because his head had slammed against the dashboard and he'd broken his neck." He looked back at me. "His head had just *turned around* like that, and I could see where a good portion of his skull had been caved in. I undid his seat belt, anyway, and even though we were sinking there was still an air pocket inside, and I tried to get to it, and that's when the semi that I'd hit came over the side of the bridge and landed on top of us. I felt my back shatter, and then it was dark and cool and quiet, and then a hand gripped my arm, and I opened my eyes and there was this this shadow floating over me. It had silver eyes, and I knew it was going to help me. 'Make sure you get my brother,' I said to it. And it pointed over to another shadow with silver eyes that was pulling Dash out of the car. They swam away so smoothly, it was kind of graceful.

"I remember looking back at the car and *seeing* our bodies still trapped inside. What was left of our bodies, anyway. It took me a long time to understand the process, how it was that our bodies are left behind—at least, for a while, and…" His words trailed off as he smiled to himself, then blinked, and—remembering his duty—pointed toward the bathroom door once again. "Get yourself cleaned up."

"I'm sorry," I said.

Hummer paused at the door once again. "What the hell for?"

"I'm sorry that you died. It must have destroyed your parents, losing both of you at the same time."

He shrugged. "We never knew. That's part of the price for being Repaired." He closed and locked the door behind him.

I went into the bathroom (which had a shower), cleaned up, found some clothes that fit (the underwear was new, still in the sealed bag), and was putting my shoes back on when I noticed that some of the clothes remaining on the rack were damaged; rips and tears that had been stitched up, dark stains on some that didn't quite come out in the wash, and some with hand-sewn, hand-lettered labels; **property of s. wilson**, **DAVE'S PANTS**, **This Jacket Belongs To: JASON.**

I wondered if the clothes I'd just put on had similar labels sewn into them, then just as quickly decided that I didn't want to know.

I heard a slight, soft *whirr* behind me, and turned around. A security camera mounted in the corner nearest the bathroom door blinked its red light and adjusted its position.

They were watching me, big surprise.

I walked toward it, and with every step I took the camera shifted its position to keep me in view.

"So these clothes," I said. "I'm guessing they were, what? Taken from the bodies and repaired, as well? Is that what all these are? Dead men's clothes?"

"Yes," said a voice behind me.

I spun around, nearly tripping over my own feet.

"Easy there, Driver," said the nightmare in the doorway. "Mustn't hurt yourself. Think of what it would do to our insurance deductibles." It laughed and rolled forward. "I'd shake your hand, but as you can see, that's somewhat problematic."

It—*he* wore no shirt and had no arms or legs, and sat in an electric wheelchair that was guided by one of those attachments that enables the user to steer by using his or her mouth. As he rolled closer I saw that he wasn't sitting in the chair at all—he was *attached* to it by a series of clamps that were soldered into the frame of the chair and disappeared into his flesh at waist level. The skin at the entry point was swollen, red, and crusted at the edges with dried blood.

"My given name is Henry," he said. "But everyone here calls me Daddy Bliss."

A series of three curved iron pipes curled out of his back and down into the wheelchair's battery. Every time the chair moved, these pipes shuddered.

"I do apologize for not dressing appropriately—one should always look one's best when greeting a new visitor—but you caught me during one of my quarterly tune-ups."

"I didn't mean to be rude. You know—staring at you."

Daddy Bliss nodded, giving me a close-up view of the matchbox-sized rectangles with electrical wires implanted in his skull. The skin of his exposed scalp was also crusty and red where it joined the metal. It was impossible to see where or to what the scalp-wires connected because they hung down his back, mixing in with a bundle of other wires that were held together by plastic clamps. What I *could* see—too clearly—were the two clear plastic bags that dangled from the metal IV pole attached to the right arm of the wheelchair. The tube from the first bag—a catheter—snaked downward and then up into his penis, which was hidden behind one of the metal waist-clamps. The bag was filled not with urine but a thick black liquid, and as I stared, I realized that the liquid wasn't going *into* the bag, it was flowing downward, into him.

"Motor oil," he said. "It seemed to me you weren't about to ask, so I thought I would get right to it."

"*Motor oil?*"

"A highly *specialized* brand, mixed with my own blood but, yes, motor oil nonetheless. The second bag contains a liquid protein supplement that helps keep me both alive and regular." To illustrate this last point, his bowels groaned, and something moist and heavy dropped into an unseen container housed within the wheelchair's lower casement.

I was glad I couldn't see it.

"My apologies," said Daddy Bliss. "But I had Thai food for dinner, and it always goes right through me. But don't worry, the casing is quite solid, you can't smell it."

"Do you ever get out of that chair?"

"Oh, goodness gracious me, *no*. I would lose my mobility, silly boy. Do you have any more questions along these lines?"

I thought of Dash, Hummer, and the foundry worker and said, "Why haven't you been repaired like the others I've seen?"

"It's a question of compatibility, my boy. Just as the human body will reject unacceptable organic tissue, the same goes for iron, steel, aluminum, plastic, any man-made alloy or other such material—it's a question of trial-and-error. Some of us have been able to be Repaired almost immediately, while others—like myself and Fairlane, who you'll be meeting later on—have to make due with more *primitive* results.

"For myself, I made the decision long ago to not attempt any further Repairs. It's an excruciatingly painful process, despite the advances we've made, and each member of our ever-growing family is given the right to say 'No more' at any point in that process. The younger ones—like Dash, Ciera, and our resplendent Sheriff Hummer—are strong, and willful, and can deal with the pain of a full Repair, which is why they can interact more openly with the outside world. Any more questions at this point?"

"No sir."

"*Sir*, is it? So respectful. I like that right down to the ground. Yes, I do." He bit down on the guidance device and turned the chair around. "Come along, Driver. There's much to show you, and time is not exactly on our side."

He rolled out the door and I followed.

10

We passed through the office and made a left, going through the same doors to the vending area that Dash had taken earlier, only now the cafeteria was empty. Daddy Bliss moved toward a set of weight-activated doors at the far end. They hissed open as soon as his wheels touched the mat in front of them.

We entered a long, brightly-lit concrete corridor.

"Our family album," said Daddy Bliss. "Feel free to stop and look at whomever catches your fancy. We were forced to eschew the traditional bound albums some time ago, for reasons I'm sure you'll come to understand."

Every inch of wall space was covered by hundreds (if not thousands) of framed photographs, each one more gruesome than the one before; a car split nearly in half by the tree it had slammed into, the body of the driver splattered across the windshield; a head-on collision between two SUVs, the vehicles so demolished it was impossible to tell where one began and the other ended, their drivers' bodies little more than pulpy smears; broken shapes of passengers who'd been thrown free, their shattered remains glistening with blood, sometimes covered in one another's internal organs; it was a photo essay of a slaughterhouse.

"As they were when the Highway People came to them," said Daddy Bliss.

"Why keep such *gruesome* reminders?"

"Because each of us must never forget our beginnings. Neither the Highway People nor—more importantly—the Road would approve." He said it with such awe and reverence I could see yet another capital 'R'.

I looked at him. "The Road?"

He gave a short nod of his head. The wires in his skull stretched as he did so. "The Road demands its sacrifices, as any self-respecting god would."

"God?" I said. "So that would make you what?"

He smiled. "Think of me as the high priest." He began turning the chair around. "Shall we, then? Get on with it?"

I stood my ground. (Not as heroic or brave as it sounds—I was still scared as hell.) "What exactly are we *getting on* with?"

He stopped, sighed, then turned back toward me. "Why must you try my patience so early on in our relationship, Driver?"

"I wasn't aware that we had a 'relationship'."

"Oh, we do, Driver. That we do."

"What's going on? What are you planning to do with me?"

"That is for the Road, and not me, to decide. I am only your guide—and you're making it dreadfully difficult for me to discharge that duty. What the Road decides, it decides between midnight and dawn. We have only a few hours remaining before your options run out. Cooperate, and you may just be on your way back home come first light. Continue to be difficult, and here you'll remain for the rest of your days." He rolled closer, glaring at me. "Do I make myself clear?"

"Yes sir."

"Again with the 'sir' business. I could get used to that."

We continued down the corridor toward a set of heavy iron doors. As we neared them, a security camera mounted over the top of the doorway made a soft *whirr*, a red light clicked on, and a set of locks within the doors disengaged.

"These doors usually require a card-key," said Daddy Bliss, "but since I have no arms, for me they will open once visual identification has been made." He looked up at the camera and smiled.

The doors opened, and I was immediately assaulted with the sounds of a factory floor at full production speed. The smells of machine grease, metal, warm plastic, dust, and a hundred other scents put my sense of smell into overdrive, and I remembered how both my parents used to smell when they came home from a hard day on the line.

I followed Daddy Bliss through the doors into a cage-style elevator. When the iron doors closed behind us, the back wall of the elevator dropped into place and the whole contraption began to rise. I reached out and grabbed two of the bars to steady myself.

"Afraid of heights, am I correct?" asked Daddy Bliss.

"Ever since I fell out of a tree in our backyard when I was five," I replied.

"You needn't worry, Driver. This elevator is perhaps the safest one in the country."

It continued to rise like a roller coaster car clack-clack-clacking up the tracks toward that drop that you just *knew* was going to send your balls up into your throat, and a few moments later the elevator stopped, shuddered, made a clack-clack-clacking of its own, and shifted forward, the top mechanisms connecting with an overhead track and pulling us forward.

"There will be a bit of a lurch in a moment," said Daddy Bliss. "It's nothing to be concerned with."

"Uh-huh."

The elevator lurched, dropping down about a foot as the whole shebang left the safety of the platform and hung suspended thirty feet above the factory floor. Once my initial panic was over, I realized that both the moving mechanism and the overhead track were solid. The ride was smooth.

Daddy Bliss grinned at me. "Better now?"

"Yes, thank you."

"Then I'll ask you to step over here and look down, please."

"I'd rather not."

"The heights business again?"

"The heights business again."

"I assure you that we are perfectly safe. Now, come here."

I moved toward the side, not once lifting my feet. Somehow it felt safer if I slid toward him.

Below us I saw three separate work areas, each one crowded with equipment and machinery that dwarfed those people working the line. I had no idea what I was looking at, what these machines were called or what function they served. I did recognize a lathe press because Dad used to operate one, and an area near one of the walls was used for wiring small circuitry chips—this I knew because Mom used to do the same thing, only she wired chips for all-night banking machines. These two things aside, I couldn't tell you what was what or what purpose it served.

The only thing that was obvious to me was that each line started with some part of a trashed automobile; a door, a dashboard, steering wheel units, under-hood components, instrument panels, floor pedals, and other parts both external and internal that I couldn't place because they'd been removed from whatever it was they'd been attached to in the first place.

The cage glided over the factory floor as the workers continued with their labors. I couldn't see what parts of the workers had been repaired from up here, save for a few people who—like Dash—had large sections of their skulls replaced with metal plates.

Daddy Bliss said, "Now here is where we see whether or not you've got half a brain, Driver. Take a good look at what's going on down there, and see if you can spot the one thing that all this busy bee-like activity has in common."

"Is this part of whatever test it is you're giving me?"

He sighed. "You mustn't think of this as a *test*, it will add far too much pressure on your nerves. Think of it more as an assessment, an evaluation, a review."

"In other words, a test."

"Have it your way, then. Now, take a good look and see if you can answer the question."

I studied the activity, though from above it was impossible to see any detail work. It wasn't until I saw one of the workers use a pair of industrial shears to strip the covering off of a control panel that I knew the answer.

"Plastic," I said. "They're removing all the plastic from what's left of the cars."

Daddy Bliss smiled. "Bravo, dear boy, bravo—though I feel compelled to point out, for the sake of accuracy, that it isn't precisely *plastic*. It's polypropylene, a form of thermoplastic. Did you know that the average car has 245.5 pounds of plastic? The ever-increasing use of plastics in automobiles helps reduce vehicle weight, thus improving gas mileage and reducing greenhouse gas emissions. A total of 4.19 billion pounds of plastic will be used in North American autos and light trucks this year, increasing to about 5.63 billion pounds within the next decade." He laughed. "All that wonderful raw material, recycled over and over again."

"Is this where you make the parts for people to be repaired?"

"Hm? Oh, goodness gracious me, no. The Repair facility is located about a mile away—in fact, I think Hummer drove by it just so you could see the place."

I remembered the worker and his taillight eye and went cold. "Yeah, I saw it."

"Excellent. *Here* is where we manufacture our goods. We produce a limited, specialized line of products here."

The cage was nearing the farthest end of the factory floor. Below us, I could see several rows of molds arranged inside shelves that were built into the walls. There was something like a large oven, and another huge contraption that looked like some kind of cooling unit, and then an area where the melted, molded, and cooled final product was cut into shape.

"Jesus..." I whispered.

They manufactured custom-made HO-tracks and cars.

I looked at Daddy Bliss. "Is this where Miss Driscoll got her track and cars? From you?"

"Her name is Road Mama, Driver, and, yes, we make every piece of track and every car to specification."

"And all of it's made from the polypropylene taken from wrecked automobiles?"

"The *track* is made from the polypropylene. The cars are made from whatever is left over from the raw materials—the automobiles—once the polypropylene has been taken. Not one piece of raw material goes to waste. It is in this way that the cycle of production and purpose keeps turning, pardon my lapsing into pathetic poeticisms."

"And alliteration," I said. "That's the second time since we've met that you've done that."

"Is it, now? I shall have to take care to watch my tongue."

The cage slowed, then shuddered once again as it moved onto another platform, disengaging from the overhead track as the front-most door rose up automatically and another set of iron doors opened before us.

We entered another brightly-lit hallway, this one with a highly-polished off-white floor and walls the same color. The iron doors closed behind us and the stink of the factory was replaced by the sharp, antiseptic smells of a hospital.

I moved alongside Daddy Bliss. "And this is…?"

"The Pre-Repair Unit."

All of the doors were closed, and there were no personnel working the floor.

We paused by one of the closed doors.

Daddy Bliss jerked his head to the side, gesturing. "Why don't you take a look through the observation window there?"

I did. I wish to hell I hadn't.

All I can say for certain is that the person lying in there was female; she could have been 17, she could have been 52—it was impossible to tell. Her massive facial injuries rendered her features almost unrecognizable as being human. Her lower body was covered by a sheet. From the ceiling there extended down a pencil-thick cable that spread out at the bottom like the wires inside an umbrella, each one attached to one of the spark plugs implanted in her skull. She jerked underneath the sheet as if in the midst of a seizure, arms and legs twitching as the spark plugs lit up in a precisely-timed sequence. Her eyes were held closed by two heavy strips of medical tape. A clear plastic tube ran from her throat into a large glass jar set on a metal table beside the bed; with each jerk, dark viscous liquid crawled through the tube and oozed into the jar. With each sequence of sparks she bit down hard on her lower lip, breaking the skin and dribbling blood down the side of her face. Finally, one of the convulsions was so violent that it knocked the sheets from over her body, exposing the metal rings that encased her torso from the center of her chest down to her knees. It looked as if she were being tortured.

I turned away, took several deep breaths to stop myself from vomiting, then looked down at Daddy Bliss and said, "Where are the nurses and doctors?"

"There aren't any. All of the medical care here is automated. The girl you saw in there is recovering from an emergency procedure. Her body rejected its new torso, so a new one is being made for her. Hopefully, we'll have better luck this time."

I looked through the window again, this time seeing that what I'd mistaken for metal rings were actually grooves in a massive cylindrical chamber encircling the center section of the bed.

"It's holding her organs in place," said Daddy Bliss as if I'd asked the question out loud. "Some of her bone structure remained intact, but not nearly enough."

"How long can you keep her alive in that condition?"

"Indefinitely. She's a stubborn case, that one. She's insisting on the full Repair, no matter how long it takes. When her Repairs are complete, we shall name her Pinto, and love her as a family should love a new member."

Next to the door was a small framed black and white photograph of a young woman that would have looked right at home in the center of a roadside memorial wreath.

"Is this her?" I asked, pointing at the photograph.

"That is how her family chose for the world to remember her, yes."

"Was this taken from a memorial?"

"Of course. That's always the second step in the Repair process."

I stared at him for a moment. "What's the first step?"

"I'd think that would be obvious—taking the soul from the shell before the body dies completely."

I looked back in at Pinto. She shuddered once more, and so did I.

"I don't…I don't understand how this is possible," I said. "How do you get their bodies? Rob the graves after they're buried? What if they're cremated?"

Daddy Bliss rolled toward me. "The bodies left at the accident scenes are of no use to us—besides, the survivors have to have *something* to grieve over and bury, don't they? We're not quite *that* heartless. No, the soul is the key. The soul, as it turns out, is a curious thing. In the initial stages of Repair, the soul's identity is still tied very closely to the individual's self-image—how they think of themselves, physically.

"At some point in everyone's life, they lock onto an image of themselves—how they looked at 27, or 32, or 45—as being, for lack of a better way to put it, the best they will ever appear, and it is *this* image that ties itself to the soul's memory. Depending on how quickly the soul is retrieved, much of that physical identity remains easily accessible, so it's not difficult to convince the soul to bring forth that physical identity once again." He smiled. "You'd be surprised how easy it is for a just-taken soul to summon flesh from the ether.

"The difficulty lies in *how long* it takes to have the soul delivered to us. In most cases, the Highway People deliver them here in a few seconds, but sometimes, when the Road has been particularly demanding on certain nights, it may take as long as two minutes before they are brought to us. When that happens, the soul has already begun its process of 'letting go' of the physical identity, and so what flesh is summoned from the ether is, well...*incomplete*. When that happens, we are forced to improvise with whatever materials are on hand."

I pointed toward the picture hanging outside Pinto's room. "Why the photos?"

"Consider them a way of checking the quality of our workmanship. Luckily, those friends and family left behind inevitably choose a memorial photograph that was taken of their loved one during this 'ideal' image time. When the soul has forgotten too much of the physical identity, we take the photograph and use it as our blueprint."

"But how can you be sure that…that you're Repairing them correctly?"

"Not to oversimplify, dear boy, but Road Mama and I decided long ago to use only three basic body types as our Repair base: endomorph—the larger and fleshier body; mesomorph—the more muscular type, and ectomorph—the slender or lean body type. These three types rarely show up in pure forms, but rather in numerous but *finite* combinations. Once we have what flesh the soul remembers, and the photograph, it's not difficult to discern which body type—or combination of body types—is required for the Repair process. Would you mind showing me your watch?"

The sudden change of subject caught me off-guard, but I did as he asked.

"Ah, how time does slip away," he said, looking at the hour. "Not that I'm *not* thoroughly enjoying our talk, Driver, but we're on a bit of tight schedule this evening. Come along."

He moved on down the hall.

I almost looked in at Pinto again, then knew I couldn't; another glance at her condition, and I might start laughing, and if I started laughing, I knew I'd never stop.

So I followed him.

I did not look through any more observation windows or at any of the memorial photographs hanging beside the doors.

We turned right at the end of the hall and moved toward a door with a frosted glass window with the words **Control Center #1** stenciled onto the glass. A security camera mounted over the door tracked our every move.

When he reached the door, Daddy Bliss once again looked up and smiled at the camera; once again, the door automatically unlocked and swung open.

We entered a medium-sized room that was taken up by expensive computer equipment. There must have been a dozen high-end machines working away in there, all of them with 25- and 40-inch LCD monitors, and all arranged on a series of wall-mounted shelves so that the sole person working the room could roll her office chair from unit to unit without banging her legs against anything.

And it appeared that Ciera—the strawberry blonde girl who'd been collecting the roadside memorials—was very busy, indeed.

Daddy Bliss gave her a quiet, loving look. "How are things going, my dear?"

"Just fine, Daddy. You're just in time for Lexington."

"Oh, *excellent*." He rolled forward. "You should see this, Driver."

"Is it going to be like back there with Pinto?"

Ciera stopped what she was doing and sighed. "Oh, Daddy! *I* wanted to show him Pinto."

"My apologies, dear, but it couldn't be helped. We were in the area and it seemed a pity to waste the opportunity." He moved closer to her. "All right—*how* angry are you?"

"I'm not angry," she said, pouting. "Just…disappointed."

"Well, this will not do, will not do at all. I can't have my favorite girl feeling this way, so here is what I propose: if the Road decrees as I think it will, then *you*, my dear, will be given the honor of *starting* the festivities."

Ciera's eyes grew wide, and then she squealed in joy and threw her arms around Daddy Bliss's neck. "Oh, Daddy, I love you *so much!*"

"As I do you, dear Ciera. As I do you."

This was the first time I got a clear look at what had been done to her arms, how the elbows had been replaced with hood hinges, her veins and remaining cartilage woven around and through the metal. No wonder they hadn't looked right earlier, even though she'd been wearing a sweater; they were each roughly six inches longer than a normal human arm was supposed to be.

She saw me staring at her, then—giving Daddy Bliss a quick and affectionate kiss on the cheek—stood up, stretching out her arms, then crossing her legs and tilting her head to the side in an imitation of the Crucifixion of Jesus. "Be honest—do these make me look fat?"

Both she and Daddy Bliss exploded with laughter.

I was still busy replaying Daddy Bliss's promise about her "…starting the festivities", so it took a moment for me to realize that, once they stopped laughing, both of them were staring at me.

"I'm sorry," I said. "I drifted off for a moment."

"You're *cute*," said Ciera. "I kinda hope you get stuck here."

"Now, now," said Daddy Bliss. "No flirting—at least, not right now. I, too, think the pair of you would make a handsome couple, but that's neither here nor there." He looked up at one of the wall clocks; there were several of them, covering different time zones. "I believe that Lexington beckons us, does it not?"

Ciera blew me a little kiss, ran her tongue quickly over her upper lip, then sat back down in her chair and rolled over to one of the computers with a 40-inch monitor. "About one minute."

"I still get goosebumps," said Daddy Bliss. "Imagine that. After all this time, and I still tingle when this happens." He looked at me. "You need to see this, Driver."

"I'd rather not."

"But I insist, *really* I do."

Not wanting to find out what happens to someone who refused his insistence, I moved over, the three of us clustering around the monitor.

"Can you split the screen?" asked Daddy Bliss. "I don't know that Driver will be able to follow otherwise." He looked at me. "No offense intended."

I said nothing. It seemed the smart thing to do.

Ciera typed in a single command, hit the **return** key, and the image on the screen split in two; on the left side, a schematic of a section of highway (presumably somewhere in Lexington, Kentucky); on the right was a live feed from a camera mounted atop what I assumed was a light somewhere along the same highway shown on the schematic.

"Okay," said Ciera, turning a smaller desk-top monitor toward us. Its screen showed a middle-aged man sitting in his living room, running two HO-scale cars around a large track that was an exact replica of the schematic. Beneath this image was a series of changing numbers and the words **Bloomington, Indiana**.

The man onscreen stopped for a moment, looked at the clock, then carefully placed two more cars onto the track at different locations; after that, he picked up a second control handset and squeezed the triggers on both. The cars on the track began moving, and at the same time four blinking lights appeared on the schematic, each one following the same path as its counterpart on this man's track.

"You might want to step back a little bit," said Ciera. "The idea is to take all this in at a glance. It'll be easier for you to see everything if you move back a foot or two."

I did as she said, and watched as **Bloomington, Indiana** increased the speed of the HO-scale cars.

As he increased the speed, the blinking lights on the highway schematic began moving faster.

As the blinking lights on the schematic moved faster, two cars became visible in the distance from the live-feed camera.

Daddy Bliss wasn't looking at the screen any longer; he was watching me. "I do believe that our Driver has figured something out."

"Oh, *God…*" was all I could get out.

When it happened, it happened quickly.

Two cars approached the camera, a Ford Explorer and a Chevy Corvette. They were one lane apart, both going at roughly the same speed. As they drove closer to the camera, two cars traveling in the opposite direction on the other side of the concrete divider zoomed into view; a Pontiac Bonneville and a Saturn Ion Sedan. The Pontiac and Saturn were going well over the speed limit. The Pontiac veered into the lane directly behind the Saturn and flashed its brights. The Saturn increased its speed, as did the Pontiac. I wondered what the hell the Pontiac driver was thinking, what he (or she, I couldn't tell) thought was going to be accomplished by this. Maybe the Saturn had done something to piss him off, and the Pontiac driver was just acting on impulsive anger. Or maybe the Pontiac was trying to get in the Exit lane and the Saturn driver was just fucking with him.

A few moments later, it didn't much matter.

The Saturn suddenly hit its brakes (or had its brakes hit *for* it). The Pontiac slammed into the back of the Saturn, crumpling its own front end and upending the Saturn, which flipped over the divider just as the Explorer came up from the other side. The Saturn landed on the hood of the Explorer, crumpling it and forcing the Explorer to slant-skid right and sideswipe the Corvette, causing the driver to lose control and spin out, the rear of the car smashing into the divider and sending the thing spinning even harder, coming to a screeching halt a second before the Explorer slammed into its side and the Saturn came off its hood to smash squarely onto the Corvette's roof.

It couldn't have taken six seconds.

The man on the smaller monitor dropped his handsets and walked over to his HO tracks, examining the four smashed, piled-up cars.

The schematic showed a single blinking light now, this one bigger than the others, and flashing a bright red.

The live feed showed only a mass of smoking, twisted, smashed, bloody metal and glass. The Pontiac had run halfway up the divider after rear ending the Saturn, and looked like a sick beast trying to climb over a rock.

After a moment, one of the Saturn's doors opened and a woman who was nothing but blood from head to heel fell out onto the highway. A moment later, several bulky shadows dislodged themselves from the night and swam toward the wreckage.

I couldn't watch any more. I turned away, closing my eyes.

A few moments later, I felt a hand on my shoulder.

"It's okay now," said Ciera. "It's over."

I opened my eyes and saw Daddy Bliss moving toward me.

"So," he said, "you've some idea now?"

I could barely find my voice, but somehow managed to do so. "One question."

"Of course."

I pointed toward the screens. "Is this…do you…"

"Take your time, Driver. Take a deep breath. There you are. Now, once more?"

"These accidents…they're not *accidents* at all, are they?"

Daddy Bliss sighed. "I think the answer to that should be obvious, dear boy. But that's not your real question, is it?"

I looked right into his unblinking eyes. "Is it just certain accidents like this one, or is it all of them?"

"Ah, direct and to the point this time. Splendid. Allow me to return the candor, Driver." He moved closer to me. "It is all of them. It has always been all of them. *All* of them."

"…oh, God…"

"So you believe?"

"…yes…"

"You've no idea how much that pleases me. It will make the rest of this *so* much easier."

I looked at the destruction on the monitor once more. "Says you…."

11

Daddy Bliss decided to skip the tour of the Repair Unit itself. "You've already seen the 'before' and 'after' of the process. The 'during' portion would be a bit of overkill at this point, I think."

We were back in the holding room, having re-traced our route through the halls and elevators. I'd almost looked in on Pinto again but closed my eyes at the last moment and just kept moving.

Someone had prepared a lovely meal for me; broiled pork chops in garlic-and-butter sauce, steamed vegetables, homemade rolls, a nice side salad with parmesan cheese and no dressing, and a generous slice of pecan pie topped with an even more generous portion of real whipped cream for dessert. A large, frosty mug of A&W Root Beer sat on a coaster, the ice cracking and rising to the top, thin beads of condensation running slow rivulets down the sides.

When we'd first entered the room, all I could do was stare at everything. If it were possible to have all of my favorite foods in one place at one time, prepared exactly the way I preferred them, then this meal was it.

"How did you know?" I asked him as I picked up the mug and sipped at the root beer.

"How did we know what?"

I stared at him. "Please don't be cute with me, sir."

He grinned. "Apologies. You want to know how we knew what to prepare, and how to prepare it?"

I looked at the food. "Or you could just tell me that you already know all there is to know about me and be done with it."

"We already know all there is to know about you. We've known since the moment you took that map from Road Mama's apartment. I'm sensing more questions coming, am I correct?"

"You have to admit, this is an awful lot to take in."

"Agreed." He glanced at the clock on the wall—a clock that had not been here earlier. "We have some time—not much, but enough.

Ask your questions but, please, do eat your food as you do so. Nova prepared the meal herself, and she is by far the best cook in town."

I picked up the knife and fork and began carving up the first pork chop. I paused with the first piece halfway to my mouth and said, "Some people might look at this—all their favorite foods prepared just how they like them—and think, 'This is a last meal.'"

His only response was to stare at me.

"I did nothing to deserve this." I popped the piece into my mouth and chewed. It was perfection.

"On the contrary," said Daddy Bliss. "The moment you took that map, you put yourself in this position—wait, that's not entirely correct. The moment you asked Mr. Dobbs to take a close look at everything on Road Mama's bedside table, you were already on your way here, you just didn't know it—ooh, that sounds so *ominous*, doesn't it? I would apologize, but I so rarely have the opportunity to indulge my flair for the dramatic."

"You were watching, even then?"

"The Highway People were watching, dear boy. They are always watching."

I stopped carving up the pork chop and stared at an empty space in the middle of the table. It wasn't quite as effective as staring at my feet, but it got results. "The bowl and the prescription bottles."

"Yes…?"

I looked at him. "I was right. They were left there on purpose, weren't they? You—or the Highway People—wanted someone to figure it out."

"'Needed' would be the more applicable term but, yes, it was the will of the Road that those items be left in plain sight. Had you kept quiet when Mr. Dobbs came back into the room, had you said nothing at all, then there might have been some doubt as to whether or not you had known. But fortunately for us, you did *not* keep quiet." He smiled. "But even if you had, you still took the map off the wall. Either way, you'd marked yourself."

"So the coroner, the mayor, the chief of police…all of them knew that Miss Driscoll—that Road Mama—had committed suicide?"

"Of course. And they also know that there are certain protocols that must be followed if and when something like this occurs."

I thought of Barb, and how she'd told me three times to be careful.

"What is it?" asked Daddy Bliss. "You have the look of someone who's just realized his lover has betrayed him."

"Barb, my lawyer. She's in on this, isn't she?"

"This may come as surprise to you, dear boy, but no, she isn't. She knows only as much as those in authority told her. But she's a sharp one, your Barbara. She suspects there's more going on than what she's been told, but she also knows enough to not speak of it too loudly, if at all. You needn't worry, Driver. Your friend did not betray you."

My hand was shaking, but I still managed to hold the fork. "Exactly how many people *do* know about you? I mean, outside of *here*?"

He thought about this for a moment, then replied: "There's an old conspiracy theory joke about what happens when a man is elected President of the United States. It is said that, as soon as he assumes office, the president is taken to a room in the basement of the White House where the people who *really* control the country sit him down in a chair and show him a film of the Kennedy assassination—not the famous Zapruder film, *another* film, shot at the same time, but this one taken from a radically different angle and much, much closer—so close, in fact, that some of Kennedy's blood spatters on the lens. Once this film has been shown to him, the president is asked, 'Do you have any questions?' To which he replies, 'Just tell me what my agenda is.'

"It's not so different with us and the people who hold office in this country. It doesn't matter if they're the president or a governor or simply the mayor of some backwater township. If they are in power, they are aware of us. And they are *very* careful with whom they choose to share this knowledge.

"This country—and arguably the world—survives because of the Road. Of course there are planes and ships and trains for transporting people and supplies, but mostly, dear boy, it is the Road that sustains us, that serves as the main artery of the economy. Delivering food, medicine, building supplies, fuel, books and newspapers, moving the sick, transporting children to and from school…ultimately, everything that enables a society to function on a day-to-day basis is made possible because of the Road. Close a single busy street in the middle of a city for even a day, and you have an immediate effect on that city's economy—people are late for work because they have to drive however-many miles out of their way, service stations see more business because of the fuel needed to make these detours, or maybe they see less, it all depends on the location of the street, doesn't it? Merchants can see either a large climb or a massive drop in their business because of a street closing. A person who is, say, suffering a heart attack—or a woman in labor—may not be able to make it to the hospital in time because of this closing. The possibilities for loss and gain are endless. And that's with just a *single* street…providing it's the *right* street.

"Now imagine what might happen if several streets, *major* streets, were all closed simultaneously for a prolonged period of time. A month. Two months. Three. *A year.* A city's economy—not to mention the well-being of its citizens—would be adversely affected in a matter of days. *Then* close enough of the right highway exits and entrances on top of that, and one could theoretically make access to a particular city or town nearly impossible. People like your mayor, your coroner, your chief of police, know all too well that the economy of their city can be destroyed if we decide to close enough streets and highway access ramps for an indefinite period of time. *That* is why they cooperate with us. You think it's the city planning commissions who decide what streets to close for construction, or where the new mall is going to be located? No, dear boy, *everything* is decided for them by the Road, and the Road's orders are delivered by the Highway People, and are then carried out by us—and, of course, our emissaries."

"Like Road Mama and that guy in Bloomington?"

"Precisely. You're not eating your meal."

I dropped my fork. "I seem to have lost my appetite."

"Then find it again. I will *not* have you return an uneaten meal to our Nova. There will be no argument on this point."

I glared at him for a moment, then picked up the fork and shoved a piece of the pork chop into my mouth. It was still perfection, and I continued to eat. It gave a sense of normalcy to things, and I needed that.

Besides, Nova was one hell of a cook. I would have liked to have told her that in person.

"How else do you ensure their cooperation?" I asked. "I mean, assuming that threatening the economy of their city isn't enough?"

"Their loved ones. Oh, don't look at me like that, Driver. No one *threatens* their friends or families. We protect them. As long as those in power cooperate, their loved ones never come to any harm while on the Road. In fact, their loved ones couldn't be hurt in an accident if they tried."

I remembered the way Sheriff Hummer's car had driven itself earlier, and had no reason to disbelieve what Daddy Bliss was telling me.

I swallowed a sip of root beer. "And if they fail to cooperate…?"

"Then our protection is lifted, and their loved ones' numbers are placed back into the order."

"The order?"

Daddy Bliss nodded toward my meal. "Do try Nova's rolls. Flaky on the outside, soft and warm on the inside. She uses just the right amount of butter."

Not looking away from his face, I took a bite from one. It practically melted in my mouth. *God* this was good food.

"The order…?" I said again.

His eyes were as cold as his voice. "The moment that you are born, Driver, you are either chosen by the Road as an acceptable sacrifice or are spared by it—that's not to say that those who are spared won't meet an even more terrible fate somewhere down the line, but for whatever reason, the Road doesn't choose them and so their fates are of no interest to us. But those who *are* chosen, those whom the Road deems an acceptable sacrifice, are given a number. It's quite a long number, actually, containing as it does the year, month, day, time, and location of death—and before you ask, yes, the *location* is also a number, albeit one that also contains letters. Every inch of highway, road, and street in this country is identified on the national grid as a specific number in a topological pattern—how do you think satellite navigation works in newer automobiles with systems that employ GPS technology? It's all broken down into numbers, dear boy. Even those sections of new road and highway that have yet to be built have a number, one only the Road knows in advance."

"So the accident I saw earlier tonight—"

"—the *occurrence*, Driver, the occurrence. There are no accidents."

"Fine—the *occurrence* I saw earlier, all of those people were predetermined to be in that place at that time since the moment of their birth?"

"Yes."

Something clicked in my head at that moment. It wasn't any kind of epiphany, not even close. I once read a line in novel that went something like, "There comes a time when the human mind can no longer deal with the amount of horror being heaped upon it, and so it all starts to become kind of funny." That's what happened to me at that moment: some small part of the rational area of my mind clicked off and all of this became oddly surreal. I went with it, and continued eating throughout the rest of our conversation, eventually finishing every bite of Nova's delicious dinner.

"So if someone's number is put back into the order, what happens if it turns out that number has already come and gone?"

Daddy Bliss grinned. "They are sacrificed immediately. If we are well past the point in the order where that number should have fallen, the very next time they climb into an automobile, they will not emerge from it alive. It causes a little extra bookkeeping for us, but it's a small price to pay for keeping the Road satisfied."

I gobbled down the second half of the roll. “So how is it that the Road came to dictate all of this?”

He stared at me for a moment. “You’re really a much more perceptive fellow than you give yourself credit for, Driver. You’ve asked a surprising amount of insightful questions this evening. One would not expect that from a person who holds your station in life.”

“I’m guessing that was meant to be a compliment?”

“It was.”

“Then thank you. Now would you mind answering my most recent insightful question?”

“Ah, yes…the ‘how’ of it all.

“Even in the midst of death, dear boy, life resonates. It seethes, trapped, waiting to be given release, to be given form. You’ve been in jail, Driver, you must have some idea to what I’m referring. You’ve been in a cell where the massed feelings of hatred, deprivation, claustrophobia, and brutalization have seeped into the very stones. One can *feel* it. The emotions resonate. It is the same when someone dies on the Road. That energy spills from their mangled bodies and is absorbed by the Road. And when a place or thing absorbs the resonating sentience of enough life, it’s only a matter of time before it achieves sentience itself. That’s why one can sense the despair emanating from the walls of a jail cell, or why you felt the death seeping from every corner of the Leonard house all those years ago. It’s not so much an unnatural phenomenon as it is what a physicist might deem an ‘unconscious confluence’ of resonating energies. *That* is how the Road came into full being.”

I nodded my head. “Okay.”

“That’s all? ‘Okay’? Just like that?”

"Just like that."

He blinked. "How utterly intriguing." He looked once more at the clock. "Have you anything further you'd like to discuss with me?"

I finished with the first pork chop and began carving up the second one, my mouth watering. "Do I have a number?"

"No, you do not. You were not deemed an acceptable sacrifice. You *were,* however, of interest to the Road, and so you were watched." He moved his chair closer to me. "I will tell you that your friend Barbara Greer *does* have a number, as do several of the employees on your crew. And your ex-wife."

I almost couldn't swallow the food, but managed to force it down. "Why tell me this?"

"Because if the Road decides about you as I think it will, you might find this information to be helpful."

"Helpful how?"

He shook his head. "Cart before the horse, and all that. We'll see if I am correct, and then proceed from there."

There was a knock on the door, and a moment later Ciera entered, carrying a phone. "It's time, Daddy. The Highway People are gathering."

I looked at him. "So the jury's coming in, is that it?"

"Indeed." He maneuvered the chair around and started toward the opened door. "You and I may not have any further time alone after this, Driver, so allow me to say that it has been a genuine pleasure getting to know you. The Road has chosen wisely with you."

"Thanks, I guess."

"You're welcome, perhaps." And with that, he rolled out the door and was gone.

"Did you two have a nice talk?" asked Ciera as she plugged the phone into the jack on the wall.

"It was very…informative."

"Cool." She set down the phone next to me and began to leave.

"Wait a second."

She turned back. "You need a refill on the root beer? We've got plenty." She giggled. "I had some earlier, though I wasn't supposed to—we got it just for you. Hope you don't mind."

"No. What I *do* mind is this." I held up the phone and turned it toward her.

It had no number keys.

"What about it?" she asked.

"How am I supposed to make a call when I can't punch in or dial the number?"

She smiled. "Operators are standing by." Then she laughed. "Sorry, I've always wanted to say that in real life but never got the chance. Just pick up the receiver when you're ready and your call will be put through. You've got about fifteen or twenty minutes now. I'll be back for you soon." She blew me a kiss and began closing the door behind her, then stopped and said, "Listen, it'd be a good idea if you didn't try to leave this room until I come back. When the Highway People call for a gathering like this, things become a bit…well, for *you*, anyway…things would be kind of confusing."

"In what way?"

She thought about this for a minute, and as she did, I caught a glimpse of the young girl she'd once been, one who was now searching for a way to express in words something for which her previous life-experience had given her no point of reference. She looked almost…innocent. If I'd been a couple of decades younger, the look on her face would have really turned me on; now it just made me feel sad and old.

Finally she said: "You ever wake up from a dream in the middle of the night and for a couple of seconds you're, like, not sure whether you're awake in your own bed or still in the dream? Some parts of the dream are so fresh in your memory that you can still see them, and for a couple of seconds it's like the dream and the real world are the same thing, only you can't tell which is which? Like you're looking at a double-exposed photograph. Does that make sense?"

I nodded. "Sure does."

"Well, if you leave this room on your own, that's what everything's going to seem like to you. You won't be able to tell what's real and what isn't."

"Why is that?"

"Because part of what holds this all together is everyone being here and doing their jobs, living their lives. But when the Highway People call for a gathering and everyone leaves their posts, there's, like, no glue, right? Things start to…come apart, change, whatever. But when we come back, it all snaps back into place. That's because we know what it's all supposed to be like. *You* don't, so everything would look *real* screwed-up to you, and you'd get lost in a hurry, and I don't think we could find you again."

I looked around the holding room. "Is that why this room is so bare? So it would be easy for me to remember what it looked like?"

"Yeah. We move around a lot—the town, I mean—and we move pretty fast. Fast like" —she snapped her fingers— "that. So it's important that you stay here in this room you know so you don't get lost in the empty places." She gave me a sweet, slightly melancholy look, blew me another kiss, and left.

I expected her to lock the door behind her to make sure I'd stay right where I was supposed to, but she didn't. She trusted me. Not that it mattered; I couldn't have found my way out of town on my own. I could maybe get myself as far as the gas station, but that'd be about it.

So I finished Nova's superb dinner, sat back in my chair, and stared at the phone, wondering who I knew who wouldn't hang up on me for calling at this hour. Maybe Brennert, but what could I tell him? Barbara Greer might not get too upset, but if she were being watched, a call from me would only draw more attention to her.

I sat forward and picked up the receiver to see if there was an operator waiting at the other end. I listened to the ringing, still having no idea who I was going to call if and when the operator answered. In the middle of the third ring the call was answered, but instead of an operator I got a moment of hiss, followed by a recorded voice-mail introduction:

"Hi, this is Dianne. I can't come to the phone right now, but if you'll leave a message…oh, you know the rest. You'll have three minutes after the beep, so don't feel like you have to talk really fast. I *hate* that, don't you? Okay, thanks for calling."

This was the first time in five years that I'd heard her voice, and it almost broke me in half; clear and musical, with a subtle South Carolina accent that caused her to end every sentence on a smoothly descending note of embarrassed laughter that snuggled down in the back of her throat and wrapped itself up in something like a purr…I could almost feel her voice with my fingertips. In those few seconds it took to listen to her message, all those parts of her that I'd purposefully chipped away bit by bit in an effort to make her just another memory came together again, and there she was: her smile, her laugh, her eyes, the smell of her in the morning, the scent of her shampoo lingering on the pillow long after she'd lifted her head, the ghost of her touch against the back of my hand, and before I could even release the breath I didn't know I was holding, the empty space in my life that had once been filled by her hummed so intensely with her absence that the last half-decade of my existence suddenly seemed inane and empty, a prolonged delusion, a vaudeville of what a life was supposed to be.

God, how I'd missed her.

Then came the beep and I began talking.

"Hi, Dianne, it's, uh…it's me."

And then it hit me: I had less than three minutes. What the hell do you say to someone under these circumstances when you've only got *three minutes*, and it might very well be the last time you ever have the chance to say anything to them? For a second I flashed upon a high school drama club production of Edgar Lee Masters' *Spoon River Anthology* that I'd been in; the director had explained to us that we needed to approach each of the monologues as that character's only chance to come back from the grave and say all the things they *wished* they'd said to everyone while they were still alive. *"Their only shot at finally making things right,"* she'd told us.

So, I thought, *just pretend you're a dead man back for a few moments from the grave. Got it? Good. Places…*

"Please don't skip over or erase this. I don't have a lot of time. Listen to my voice. I'm not drunk, okay? What I am is in a lot of trouble, and I don't know if I'm going to be…ah, hell, Dianne. I never stopped loving you, and I've never stopped missing you. I was a jerk—no, wait, that's not quite right, is it? I was cruel and selfish and cold, and I've never forgiven myself for it. Don't worry, I'm not about to ask for your forgiveness, though I'd bet you *would* forgive me if I asked. You were always so compassionate, and thoughtful, everything any man who had the brains God gave an ice cube would want or hope for. But me? I blew it. And I want you to know how sorry I am. I hope that whoever you're with now treats you with all the respect and affection you should have gotten from me.

"You told me after the divorce hearing that you figured I'd go on and live my life like you'd never been a part of it. I tried. And it worked for about a week. Then one morning I got up and started making my lunch for the day and realized halfway through that I was packing yours, as well, like I used to some days, remember? I'm standing there in the middle of kitchen looking at a tuna fish sandwich and wondering if I used enough mayo—you still like lots of mayo on your tuna fish?—anyway, I'm standing there with this goddamn sandwich and realize that you're not going to be eating it, and I started…well, I kinda lost it, and I hugged the sandwich to my chest and squashed it all the hell over my shirt…it was one of those mawkish moments that always used to make you laugh when you saw them in a movie. It was really pitiful." I looked at the clock; I had less than a minute.

"I want you to know something, Dianne. You were the love of my life—you *are* the love of my life, and whatever happens tonight, even if I never see or hear from you again, my soul was blessed because you were once a part of my life, and even though I didn't treasure it at the time like I should have, I treasure it now, and wish to God I'd have the chance to treasure it—to treasure *you*—again. But I don't think that's going to happen. Just know that everything you did, all you tried to give to me, all of it *mattered*, all of it. And whatever happens after I hang up, if this is it, I want you to know that my last thought will be of you and how you made my world rich, even if I was too much of an idiot to appreciate it at the time.

"*I love you*. I always will. I just…I just wanted to thank you for all you gave to me when we were together.

"And it just occurred to me that all of this must sound melodramatic as hell, and I'm sorry. It's been an…odd couple of days. But it's almost over now. I love you. Be happy, and never let yourself think that any part of what happened was because of you. You were wonderful—shit, you were *perfect*. I was an asshole. I didn't deserve you. This isn't self-pity, hon, it's just plain old regret. Six of one, half-dozen of the other, I know.

"Good-bye, Dianne. I love you. Think about using a little less mayo in the tuna fish, okay? I hear it's not good for the cholesterol. You may quote me."

The beep sounded again, I hung up, covered my eyes with my hands, and wept quietly for a minute or two.

The lights flickered and I looked up just as Ciera opened the door. "It's time." She stared at me. "Are you okay?"

Wiping my eyes, I shook my head, then said, "Just ducky, thanks."

"Nobody *wants* you to get hurt, Driver."

"So I keep hearing." I wiped my eyes once again, let out a breath, and rose.

We stared at each other for a moment.

"So?" I asked. "I take three giant steps, or what?"

"I wish you wouldn't be so mean to me."

"I didn't think I was."

She glanced down at the floor for a second, then back up at me. There was some genuine hurt in that gaze. "I keep trying to be nice, but you act like you don't like me very much."

"*Like* you? I don't even *know* you. Until a few hours ago, I had no idea you or anyone else in this place even existed! All I knew was that I was supposed to deliver a body so the family could bury it, that's all. Now, suddenly, I'm right smack in the middle of something pretty seriously goddamn scary, I might be dead before the sun rises, and you're getting defensive about my bad manners?"

Her eyes began tearing up. "Please don't yell at me."

"What the fuck would you *do if you were in my position?"*

"Please stop yelling."

I opened my mouth to really let her have it, then her words—*Please stop yelling*—echoed back, only this time it was Dianne's voice I heard speaking them, as it had so many times during the course of our marriage whenever I had been made aware of my shortcomings and was looking for someone to blame, usually her.

Please stop yelling. Oh, hon…

"I'm sorry," I said to Ciera, stepping forward and putting a hand on her shoulder. "I'm not mad at you. I'm just…mad."

"Okay," she said, not meeting my gaze.

"Hey?"

She looked up at me.

"What's your name—your *real* name?"

A single tear slipped from her eye and slid a slow path down her cheek. "I don't remember."

"Really?"

“Really. Only Road Mama and Daddy Bliss remember their real names. The rest of us, we kinda…don’t bring them with us when we come back.”

“How old were you?”

“I would have been twenty-one on my birthday.”

“Christ…I’m so sorry.”

“Not your fault. I really like you, Driver. It’s been a long time since…well, since a new guy’s been here who’s still got all of his face and stuff.” She shrugged. “I get lonely sometimes.”

I touched her face, using my thumb to wipe away the tear. “How bad is it, being trapped here?”

She stared at me for a moment, blinked, then gave her head the slightest shake. “I’m not trapped her. *None* of us are.”

“You stay here *by choice?*”

“Yes. Everyone here is given that choice. The Highway People bring them back, and if you choose to stay, then your Repairs begin.”

I *really* couldn’t get my head wrapped around this one. “But… for God’s sake, *why* would you choose to stay here and take part in all of this?”

“The people we leave behind. If we choose to stay, they are protected. I mean, it’s not like it can be *all* the people we leave behind, but our immediate family and closest friends, they’re okay.”

“Their numbers are withdrawn from the order?”

“If they *have* a number, yes. If, like, my sister didn’t have a number—and she didn’t—then I got to pick an extra friend.”

“How long do you have to stay here?”

"Until the people we pick die of natural causes, or however it is they *do* die. Just not by the Road. Once they've all passed on, then we can follow them."

I tried doing a little arithmetic in my head—if you picked five people, and the youngest was only twelve, then how long…?—then realized it was pointless. She was talking about a *long* time, no matter how you looked at it.

"Can I ask you stupid question?"

She smiled. "You can ask me anything. I won't think it's stupid."

"How do you get by on a day-to-day basis? How do you stay sane?"

She thought about this for a moment, and then shrugged. "Like everybody else does, I suppose. You go to work when you're supposed to, you do your job, then you go home, eat dinner, maybe watch some TV or put in a movie. Hang out with friends. Y'know… normal stuff."

"Watch TV or movies?"

"Uh-huh."

"Hang out with friends?"

"Uh-huh…?"

"I guess I'm asking…what do you do for fun? What do you do to relax?"

"I like to take walks."

For a moment I thought she was joking, then just as quickly realized she wasn't.

She took hold of my hand, leaned up, and kissed my cheek. "We really need to get going."

"Ciera, please, *please* tell me what's going to happen."

"I can't. I could get into a lot of trouble if…" She broke off, stared at me, and smiled. "Let me ask you something, okay?"

"Okay…?"

"Am I prettier than Dianne?"

No way was I going to lie to her—she was the closest thing to an ally that I had (and something told me she'd know instantly if I tried bullshitting her)—but maybe I could respond without actually answering the question.

I touched her cheek and said, "I think you're beautiful."

"Thank you. You're going to race Fairlane."

I remembered Daddy Bliss's words from earlier—*Some of us have been able to be Repaired almost immediately, while others—like myself and Fairlane, who you'll be meeting later on—have to make due with more* primitive *results*—and felt myself shudder. If Fairlane had to make do with results even *worse* than Daddy Bliss's, I wasn't sure I wanted to meet him at all, so saith the King of Understatement.

"A race?"

She nodded. "The Road decided long ago that a race was the most direct and just way to settle a matter."

"What happens if I win?"

She almost giggled. "Silly—you get to leave and go home."

"And if I lose?"

She stared at me for a moment, and then threw her arms around my neck and planted a kiss on me that would have killed a kid half my age; as it was, it left me weak in the knees.

"Then," she said, "you and I can be together."

So it was that simple; win, and I could leave; lose, and here I'd remain. It seemed almost *too* simple, but at the time I didn't dwell on it. I was only interested in getting the hell out. In one piece, if possible.

She took hold of my hand and led me from the holding room, through the offices, and to the front doors. I looked out the windows and saw a long, dark limousine parked at the curb, engine purring. Ciera opened the door and out we went. As we neared the limo I saw, at last, how it was that Sheriff Hummer's car was able to drive itself; a deep groove ran all along the center of both street lanes: the whole city was built on a gigantic HO track.

Ciera opened the back door of the limo and held my hand until I was seated inside.

"This is as far as I go," she said. "I have to do a couple of things to get ready, but don't worry, I'll see you there in a few minutes." She started to let go of my hand and I did something that surprised both of us: I tightened my grip and put my free hand on top of hers.

"What is it?" she asked.

"I don't want to let go just yet."

She gave me a tender smile and nodded her head. "I can hang for a minute."

"Good."

I sat there trying to steady both my breathing and the beating of my heart. Ciera neither moved nor spoke, just kept hold of my hand until I was ready to let go.

"Thank you," I said.

"You're welcome. Tell you something weird—I kinda hope you win, but I also hope you don't, you know?"

An idea came to me. "You could come with me."

"*What?*"

"You and me. We get the meat wagon and hightail it out of here."

She pulled in a breath, held it, then released it with a soft little moan as she leaned in and kissed me again. "Do you have any idea how tempting that is?"

I sure hoped so. Shame on me.

"But you know I can't. I couldn't do that to my family and friends. But thank you for asking." She pulled her hand from my grip and closed the door, which locked automatically.

The limo pulled away, and I looked through the back window, watching her stand there in the street until the car turned a corner and she was gone.

Strange as it might sound, I missed her.

I looked up front to see that the divider window was up; it was tinted, so I couldn't make out anything about the person driving. I looked around until I found the intercom button, pressed it, and said: "Can you lower the window, please?"

There was a soft click, followed by a low, steady hum, and the window glided downward. There was no one driving. I should have known.

There was, however, a small television mounted on the dashboard, and as the window finished lowering, the screen flickered to life and I was looking at Daddy Bliss's face.

"This is a pre-recorded message, Driver, so please don't do anything so pointless and predictable as talking back to the screen. They lock people up for that sort of behavior.

"I'm fairly certain that you've by now managed to charm some information from our dear Ciera—I was, in fact, counting on it. So let's proceed on that assumption, shall we?

"You are being driven to the only stretch of road in our fair metropolis that is smooth blacktop from beginning to end. A three-mile straightaway that my children long ago named 'Daddy's Dead Run'. A bit over-the-top, I know, but their hearts were in the right place and I've never been able to bring myself to tell them that I think it's a silly, melodramatic name, but what is one to do?

"Once this limousine—and isn't it a *lovely* vehicle? You should help yourself to some snacks and the wet bar, both are well-stocked. Now, where was I? Ah, yes.

"Once this limousine comes to a stop, you will be taken to your vehicle for this evening's contest. You will be driving a car that I personally chose for you. I call it 'The Ogre.' Yes, I know—I have the *gall* to make fun of 'Daddy's Dead Run' and then name a car 'The Ogre'? It's the little contradictions in one's character that makes one fascinating to others. An enigma, so to speak.

"'The Ogre' was a 1964 Triumph Spitfire in its previous life. Allow me to gloat a bit of its history—after all, I designed and supervised its metamorphosis myself, so I think I've earned the right to boast.

"I began with a Spitfire frame that was made ready for a Chevy V-8 engine, Muncie transmission, and modified Corvette rear suspension. When the chassis was complete—with engine, transmission, rear suspension and third member, brake lines, front suspension with stock rack and pinion steering, as well as new body-mounts—the body from the stock Spitfire was prepared and set on the frame. The electrical systems were re-established and the bonnet added. Its present engine is a 383 Stroker. On the Dyno, she checked out at 470 horsepower and 500 ft-lbs of torque. This a small but very powerful car you'll be climbing into, Driver. It has a maximum speed of 180 miles per hour, and goes from 0 to 90 in just under ten seconds.

"For the first ten seconds of the race, both The Ogre and Fairlane's vehicle will be under the sole control of The Road. Once you have passed from the sight of the crowd, control of the vehicles will be given over to you. I trust you can drive a shift. If not—well, then, this could be a short but spectacular contest.

"You have a few minutes before you reach your destination, dear boy. Why not raid the refrigerator and wet bar? Godspeed, Driver. No pun intended."

And with that, the screen snapped off.

I looked out the window and saw the lights reflecting from the massive car-cubes along Levegh Lane in the distance, and realized that these dead piles rose so high they could be probably be seen from any place in the city.

I wondered if, very soon, the smashed corpse of the Ogre would be added to them for future Repair material.

12

FADE IN: A seemingly endless stretch of smooth two-lane blacktop emptying into shadows. Crowds of people line both sides of the road, the men looking tough while clutching at their bottles of beer, the women looking anxious while clutching at the filtered tips of their cigarettes, and the kids—especially the really young ones—looking like they aren't sure *how* they should be feeling while they clutch at the hands or coats of the tough beer drinkers and anxious cigarette smokers.

…and this is where we came in, isn't it?

I climbed out of the limo and saw the Ogre parked in the left lane up ahead, Sheriff Hummer leaning against the driver's-side door. He saw me, gave a little wave, and gestured for me to join him.

I kept glancing at the crowd as I approached him, but after a few seconds of that realized it wasn't the best idea; the people who comprised this crowd—men, women, children (*God,* the children…)—were all Repaired to varying degrees, and the fusion of flesh and metal, rather than repulse me as it had before, now seemed to possess an organic *correctness* that I was suddenly all too willing to accept as being normal…or what passed for normal, here. One little girl who couldn't have been more than seven years old smiled at me, displaying a mouthful of spark plug tips that took the place of her teeth. She seemed so proud of that smile, like she was showing off. I smiled back at her, and she blushed.

Don't look at them, I told myself. *If you don't look, then they're not there.*

Pitiful, I know, but it worked. They were shadows, props, decorations on the periphery, not real, not flesh and bone (*and metal and steel,* said the voice in the back of my head), and maybe, if I concentrated hard enough, I could Zen-out of this whole mess for a few moments.

"You seem tense," said Hummer.

I looked up at him but couldn't think of anything to say.

Then he did something that surprised me; he stepped forward and put a hand on my shoulder and said, "You'll be fine. It's almost over."

I heard the grinding of a large engine in the distance behind us, and as I turned the crowd broke into wild shouts and applause. More lights came on, illuminating the road, and a few seconds later the object of their adulation rolled into sight.

A great semi tractor-trailer crawled out of the darkness, pulling a car-cube, smaller than the ones I'd seen before but still fairly massive. Atop the cube four large torches burned, flames snapping against the night, one set at each corner, and in the middle of it all was a raised platform. Daddy Bliss sat there, the wheels of his chair held in place by clamps attached to the base. Large concert speakers were positioned at the sides of the platform, angled outward. Ciera stood at Daddy Bliss's side. She'd changed clothes; she was now dressed in a paisley skirt and tight short-sleeved sweater, her blonde hair pulled back into a ponytail, a scarf tied around her neck. She held a long red kerchief in each of her hands.

The truck crept by, rumbling and growling like a constipated dinosaur, then began a slow, wide turn, moving forward, then back, a little to the left, forward again, the driver doing an impressive job of reversing, until, finally, the car-cube was well off the road and at an angle facing the crowd.

Ciera walked to the side of the cube and pushed something over the edge; a long rope ladder that reached to the ground. She turned, blew a kiss toward Daddy Bliss, and began descending.

Daddy Bliss smiled—a celebrant at the beginning of Mass—and the crowd's cheering grew even louder. He smiled, nodded his head a few times, then cleared his throat; amplified by the speakers, it sounded as if a section of the ground were splitting open.

The crowd fell silent.

"My children," said Daddy Bliss.

And the crowd exploded once again. Daddy Bliss waited until the roar died down, but it took a minute; Ciera was already on the ground before he started speaking again.

"My children. As you know, our dear Road Mama has been returned to us, and is, as I speak, being Repaired. She will be back among us soon. For that, we have Driver to thank."

The crowd erupted once more, some of them calling out my name—or, rather, the word, *"Driver! Driver!"*

"The Road," said Daddy Bliss, "has granted us this contest—this *trial*, if you will—to see whether or not Driver is, indeed, worthy."

Worthy of what? I thought.

"Give praise to the Road. Give thanks to the Highway People. They provide, they sustain, they bless us and watch over our loved ones under their protection."

The crowd as one looked downward and began muttering quiet thanks. Even Hummer removed his hat and bowed his head in prayer.

"Driver," said Daddy Bliss.

I looked up toward him.

"You have done well for us, and have our thanks. You still have many questions, this I do realize. Know that they will be answered soon."

I nodded.

"Very well, then," he said, clearing his throat once more. When he spoke again, his voice was louder, powerful, commanding. "Release Fairlane." Then he looked at me and grinned. "Sounded somewhat *ominous* didn't it? Apologies. 'Release Fairlane.' Not quite '…let slip the dogs of war,' I'm afraid."

The crowd cheered, but this time I could hear some genuine anxiety at the edges of the sound.

And then something so incredibly absurd happened that I couldn't even laugh at it, as much as it *demanded* to be laughed at: the concert speakers erupted with the opening chords of AC/DC's "Highway To Hell" and the crowd as one turned to face the road behind me.

"I'm dead, aren't I?" I said to Hummer. "I got in a wreck on my way out of town and all of this is just some fucked-up hallucination that my subconscious has dredged up while my life trickles away."

Hummer grinned, and then backhanded me across the mouth. "Did that *feel* like an hallucination?"

"That *hurt!*"

"Sorry. Seemed the best way to get the point across, all things considered."

I shook it away, which wasn't easy—he had one helluva powerful swing. When I was able to gather myself together and stand fully upright, I was looking down the darkened road at something that appeared to be a small bonfire, only it was moving.

The music became louder as the whole band kicked in, the *thump-a-thump-thump* of the base and drums shaking the ground under my feet, and the bonfire grew brighter, wider, and closer.

Ciera appeared at my side. "Fairlane is…I'd guess you'd call him…I dunno…The Road's guard dog. Does that make sense?"

"Not really." I tried to grin at her and didn't quite make it. "I guess I could use some reassuring words."

"Then try this," said Hummer. "If you took every instance of violence, death, pain, and destruction that have occurred on the roads and highways of this country and forced them all together so that they'd have a single form, it would be Fairlane."

I stared at him for a moment. "I think we need to compare notes about the definition of 'reassuring.'"

"He's the closest thing to an actual demon you'll ever meet," said Ciera, taking hold of my hand. "And he's got terrible table manners."

Hummer nodded. "Not a pretty motherfucker, that's for sure."

"Plus he cheats," said Ciera.

I could make out a shape in the middle of the flames; the outline of a car's body, the massive hunched shoulders of the driver, the glint of light off metal and chrome.

The flames, I now realized, were coming from two sources: the back tires and the exhaust pipes that ran along the sides of the car. The cloud of flame, smoke, and exhaust moved up to the right lane and came to a stop right beside the Ogre. I blinked, shielding my eyes, hacking against the fumes, and waited for the cloud to clear.

I have no idea if what happened next was just a coincidence or something that had been previously choreographed to unnerve me, but until the day I die I'll swear that the cloud of smoke and exhaust lifted at the exact moment the song stopped.

And there he was. My opponent for the evening's festivities. I couldn't take him in all at once, that would have been too much, so I looked at the car first; at least I could get my head wrapped around that.

When I was a kid, I used to collect and build model cars. I tended to favor models of older cars because their shapes were so varied and cool—not like the generic stuff I saw on the roads then and still see now. One of my favorite models had been a Revell kit of a 1934 Ford High Boy Rumble Seat Roadster. To me, it was the single *coolest-looking* car I'd ever seen—forget that I'd never actually seen the real thing, I knew Cool when I saw it.

And this car was Cool. Same make and model, only the back end had been jacked up and the tires replaced by wide, dangerous-looking slicks. The body—what was left of it, anyway—was a fierce, bright, almost terrifying shade of red. The exhaust pipes that ran along the sides of the car covered the entire length of the body and then some, curling slightly outward at the ends. The front grille and headlights were still in place, but the rest of the body between them and the windshield had been removed to make room for an engine that was more like a gigantic chrome cobra than anything that functioned under the laws of internal combustion, its body coiled and tense, its hood expanded, ready to strike. It would not have surprised me if a forked tongue had shot out for a moment.

And then the cobra roared, just once, spitting smoke and sparks. Fairlane wanted my attention. I had no choice but to look at my opponent.

His skin—what there was of it—had the gray fish-belly pallor of something spoiled, and his head was disproportionately large for his body; like Dash, part of his skull was visible where the scalp had been torn away and cauterized at the edges. Thick strands of long, greasy, dark hair hung down the back of his head, tied into something that was supposed to be a ponytail but looked more like a section of putrid intestine left dangling for the elements to feast upon. He still had his own eyes, after a fashion: each was embedded into the center of a cone-shaped floodlight welded into the sockets. His nose was a knot of mashed tissue that leaked a thick, brown substance onto his upper lip. Every few seconds he would smile, allowing the liquid to spatter down onto his long, dark tongue that lolled around like that of a particularly happy or stupid puppy, never disappearing completely into his mouth. Something about the texture and shape of the thing demanded closer attention, and when it flopped fully out of his mouth a second time, I realized that the tongue was maybe one-third human tissue; the rest of it was a fan belt onto which the organic tissue had been attached.

Fairlane must have seen the realization hit me, because his face began to split in half as he smiled, displaying a mouth crowded with full-sized spark plugs that had been jammed in to replace his teeth, both on top and bottom. He chortled—that's the only word for it—and clicked his teeth together; a series of bouncing blue electrical currents danced around his smile. I wondered if the little girl I'd seen earlier was his daughter or niece. Maybe she was just a fan and was paying tribute to her hero.

Hundreds of metal strips were mixed in with the flesh of his arms, and several twisted license plates had been used to good advantage in replacing the pectoral muscles of his chest, but his hands were the most unnerving thing about him; long, wide, with quadruple-jointed fingers, each hand was equal parts meat and metal, with small silver hinges used in place of bone joints. One hand was fused to the steering wheel at the ten o'clock position, while the other was fused to the gearshift.

"Told you he was ugly," said Hummer.

"No," I whispered. "It'd take the *light* from ugly ten thousand years to reach him."

Fairlane chortled again, this time throwing back his head, his tongue flailing through the air.

Ciera took hold of my hand. "You need to get in your car now."

I nodded at her and crossed back to the vehicle, opening the door, climbing inside, and then buckling up—more out of habit than any belief that doing so was going to keep me safe.

"Good luck," said Ciera.

"Wait a second, please."

"What is it?"

"How…I mean…what's at the end of this road?"

"All of us—or we *will* be. You'll see." She leaned down, gave me a quick kiss, and then walked about ten yards ahead, stopping in the middle of the road and raising her arms. I stared at the red kerchiefs and tried once again to Zen-out of this whole freak show.

"On your marks," she shouted, her arms now raised to their full height, the crowd silent, wide-eyed, leaning forward.

Fairlane gunned his engine. I tightened my grip on the steering wheel. Ciera gave us both a smile that might have been radiant in any other place, under any other circumstances. "*Get set…*"

Her grip tightened on the kerchiefs in her hands. In a moment, she'd swing down those impossible arms in a swift, decisive arc, and off we'd go.

I closed my eyes and took a deep breath, wondering how long I'd be missing and dead before anyone took serious notice of my absence. It was quite the revelation, it was, to realize that out of all my friends…I didn't really have any.

"GO!" Ciera screamed, snapping down both arms simultaneously.

And we had a race.

13

I didn't have to touch anything for the first ten seconds because, as Daddy Bliss had told me, the Road was in control. My rear tires spun madly for a second or two, screaming burned rubber and churning up a lot of smoke, and then the car shot forward, slamming me back against the seat. Fairlane gunned it—or, rather, the Road gunned it *for* him—and flew ahead, but a few seconds later, just as the crowd disappeared from my rear-view mirror and the safety railings began, control of the vehicles was returned to us and I gripped the wheel, shifted, and floored the accelerator, coming up fast on him.

For a few seconds, we were side-by-side, both of us increasing speed, both of our cars shuddering, both of us being followed by bulky overhead shadows that finally swept down, causing us to hunch so they couldn't touch us, and just as quickly as they had appeared, the Highway People vanished and we got back to business.

And that's when Fairlane began cheating. He slant-drove across my front and squealed into my lane. I resisted the impulse to brake and instead sped up, ramming into his rear bumper; once, gently; the second time, not so much; and then with everything the car had, taking off part of his rear bumper and slewing him back into his own lane and against the railing where he scraped along, throwing off sparks for about a hundred yards. Some of the sparks flew toward my face, a couple of them landing on my cheek and burning the skin, but it was quick, the wind saw to that, and the pain kept me focused, kept my grip tight on the wheel, and I ran up alongside Fairlane, keeping him pinned between my car and the railing, and he was screaming, and I was laughing in panic, and when another set of sparks came spitting over against my face I jerked the wheel to the left, shot back into my lane, and surged forward.

It didn't take Fairlane long to right his vehicle and close the distance between us, but at least now he'd gotten the idea and remained in his own lane, and pretty soon we were side-by-side again—

—and that's when I discovered that Fairlane wasn't the only person here who cheated, because I looked ahead and saw the flashing visibar lights of the Sheriff's Department cruiser coming at us, roaring down on top of us, right the fuck smack in the middle, it would hit us both unless one of us did something, and I heard myself screaming "*A fucking game of CHICKEN? This all boils down to a game of CHICKEN?*" but Fairlane either didn't hear me or didn't care because he moved closer to me, so I returned the favor, our cars pressing against the other's side, neither one of us moving to get out of the cruiser's way—there was nowhere to go, the railings made sure of that—but whoever was driving the cruiser wasn't budging, just kept barreling down on top of us, and when I saw the lights of the burning torches flicker in the distance I knew we were almost done, this was it, now or never, and I figured, fuck it, I didn't have to prove my nerve to anyone, so I took a chance and stood on the brake, spinning over into the right lane, but Fairlane didn't follow suit, he just kept burning forward, looking back over his shoulder at me and laughing, and when he turned back toward the road it was too late, the cruiser was right there, and the two vehicles impacted at over a hundred miles an hour; the cruiser caught it hard in the left front, went up on its side, ricocheted, spun out, and walloped into the railing a twisted mass of steel, flames, and shattered glass. Fairlane was horizontal across the center and caught a shattering side punch from the cruiser as it spun out; he hit the railing, spun out a second time, flipped onto his side, and then scraped along for a few yards until he flipped tail-over onto his top, snapping his neck and sliding to a stop, leaving a long, wide, dark, wet trail behind as the cruiser caught fire, sputtered once, and then blew apart like an M-80 tossed into a can of kerosene.

I stared at the destruction for a few seconds, then put the car in gear, floored it, and shot through the flames and debris to cross the finish line to wild, deafening cheers. True to Ciera's word, everyone and everything that had been at the beginning of the road were now here at the end.

I slammed on the brakes and threw open the door. I couldn't get out of that car fast enough. Staggering back toward the finish line, I watched as Fairlane tore himself from his burning vehicle and stumbled out into the middle of the road, both arms missing from the elbows down, spurting blood, his head twisted at an impossible angle, black smoke swirling from his charred, sluicing flesh.

He shook his stumps at me, and then began to dance as the concert speakers once again began blasting "Highway To Hell."

Why aren't you dead? I thought.

"Because you can't kill a demon," said Hummer, stepping up beside me and putting a hand on my shoulder. "Don't worry about Fairlane. He digs the pain. Always has. Any excuse for more Repairs makes him happy."

I spun around and surprised him with an uppercut to the jaw that knocked him squarely on his ass.

"Who was driving the goddamned cruiser?" I screamed.

"Nobody," he replied, massaging his jaw and spitting out a small glob of blood.

"Why didn't you warn me?"

"Because I didn't know, all right? None of us did. The Road gets a wild hair up its ass sometimes. It decided that it wanted someone to bleed, so…." He touched his jaw again, winced, and then stuck out his arm. I helped him to his feet and fully expected him to slug me into the next decade.

"Nice punch you got there," he said. "So now we're even."

"Driver!" called Daddy Bliss from atop the car-cube. "You have, indeed, proven yourself worthy."

"Of *what?*" I shouted back at him.

"Of the Road's trust, and our family's respect and affection."

Ciera pulled up alongside me in the meat wagon, got out, and handed me the keys. "You did good, you know that, right?"

I could not find any words. The full impact of what had just happened hit me all at once, and my legs turned to rubber. She helped me into the driver's seat, smoothing down my hair and laying her hand against my cheek. "I really hope I get to see you again someday."

I looked at her, swallowed once, and finally found my voice. "What happens now?"

She tilted her head to the left, indicating the darkened road ahead. "You go home. Just drive straight for a little while, and you'll be fine."

"Just…drive. That's it?"

"That's it."

A small orange-red stain began to spread across the horizon. The crowd began to disperse.

"Time's up, Driver," said Daddy Bliss. "A new day with new responsibilities awaits us all. Off with you, dear boy; off with you."

Ciera closed the door, kissed her finger tips, and pressed them against my lips.

I started the meat wagon and drove away, never once looking in the rear-view mirror.

It took only a few minutes before the sunlight was right in my eyes. I blinked, slowed down, and dug around until I found a pair of sunglasses on the passenger-side floor. I knew they hadn't been there when I left Cedar Hill. Ciera or someone else had known that I'd be driving into the rising sun, and so left them for me.

Ten minutes. I drove for only another ten minutes before I saw the exit sign for Cedar Hill. I took the exit, turned right—

—and found myself on 21st Street.

I braked, looking around, confused. There was no traffic at the moment, no early-morning joggers on the sidewalks, no bicycle riders cruising along the curb…nor was there any sign of the exit I'd just taken. My guess is, had anyone been there to see, it would have looked like the meat wagon had just appeared out of thin air, and me with it.

Tired—Christ, I was suddenly so tired. And *hungry*. It felt like I hadn't eaten in days, despite the meal Nova had prepared for me earlier.

Do something normal, I thought. *Something banal.*

So a breakfast at Bob Evans it would be.

I'd completely forgotten about the cash I still had and so drove to my bank to get some money from the ATM. I withdrew thirty dollars and was walking back to the meat wagon when I glanced down at the receipt to check my balance and damn near tripped over my own feet.

According to the receipt in my hand, my checking account had a balance of seventy-five thousand dollars. I went back to the ATM, inserted my card, and asked for a checking account balance once more.

Still seventy-five grand.

I checked my savings account: seventy-five thousand.

I suddenly didn't have much of an appetite.

14

A brown, business-sized envelope was taped to the door to my apartment. It had no address, no return address, no stamp; only a single, handwritten word: **Driver**.

I opened it and removed the single-page letter inside.

Driver:

> You needn't worry about the government or the IRS becoming too interested in your sudden financial windfall. No one asks questions when we tell them not to.
>
> You will serve us for one year, until such time as Road Mama has completed her Repair process and can assume her duties once again. Understand that for the entirety of this year, no one close to you will be in any danger from the Road.

Upon completion of your duties, you will receive an additional deposit in each of your accounts equal to what you found waiting there this morning. You will be what was once referred to as "comfortable".

You will find instructions waiting for you inside. Your first assignment is scheduled for 9:45 p.m. this evening. This time and this time only, the track has already been assembled for you. Expect a delivery of more material Monday morning, and again on Thursday.

You're a bright fellow; you'll catch on soon enough.

Ciera sends hugs and kisses. Isn't that sweet?

I tucked the letter inside my pants pocket, unlocked the door, and stepped inside.

A massive HO track was set up in the middle of my living room. Five large boxes, containing what I assumed was more track, were stacked against the far wall. Miss Driscoll's—Road Mama's—incredible computer system was already in place on a new desk, plugged in, and running. Several large maps hung from the walls. And a box of multi-colored, thumbnail-sized foil stars waited on the coffee table.

I closed the door behind me. It clicked into place with the finality of a coffin lid being lowered.

That was nearly four months ago. Since then, I have set up over a dozen track configurations and orchestrated three times as many accidents, all according to the system, which I am still learning.

On the first day of each week I receive a list of numbers, which I then enter into the system so that the mapping and track configurations will be precise. I then construct the tracks accordingly, and wait for the delivery of the HO vehicles.

I keep exact records. So far I have choreographed the deaths of nearly one hundred people. It took me a while to figure out the star system, but I did it: silver stars are used to mark those who were injured in a wreck; blue stars are to mark those whose injuries will eventually result in their deaths, be it weeks, months, or years from the initial accident; and the gold stars—you guessed it—are for those fatalities that occur at the scene.

I have begun going to hobby stores in my spare time—what little there is of it—and buying decorations for the tracks; houses, stores, trees, human figures, dogs, cats, rabbits, whatever strikes my fancy. I understand now why Miss Driscoll went to such lengths to make her tracks more attractive, more life-like: you don't get to see the actual outside world very often, so you do your best to recreate it. It helps. Not much. But some.

I read an on-line article a few days ago that said by the end of this decade, something like two-thirds of the cars manufactured in the United States will come equipped with some form of GPS technology, and by 2021 *every* car in the country will have it. So the Road will always be able to find you when your number comes up.

The more I come to understand how precise this system is, the more I find myself admiring it. And hating myself for it.

Dianne never called me. I'm guessing she erased the message when she heard my voice. I can't blame her. I still miss her. I always will.

I quit working for Brennert. He was pissed but, being the type of guy he is, he didn't let it show. He told me he understood if I was feeling burned out, and if I ever changed my mind and wanted to come back to the job, it'd be there waiting for me.

Before I hung up, I finally asked him: "Do you ever think about the Leonard house?"

"Every day," he said.

"I was always sorry about the way Mark and I treated you that night."

"I know."

"Doesn't help much, does it?"

"Not a goddamned bit."

Click.

I did some digging on-line one night—a free night for me, which doesn't happen very often—and found something interesting.

I'd been thinking about what Ciera had said about Daddy Bliss and Road Mama, how they were the only two who remembered their real names, and I began wondering if maybe there was something out there in the ether of cyberspace that might tell me *something*.

It turned out to be a lot easier than I'd thought. I just entered the words **Driscoll** and **Cars**, then **Bliss** and **Cars**. I figured that might be a good way to begin.

Both searches pretty much started and ended right there.

On August 17, 1896, in London, Bridget Driscoll, age 44, became the world's first person to be killed in an automobile accident.

As she and her teenage daughter crossed the grounds of the Crystal Palace, an automobile belonging to the Anglo-French Motor Car Company and being used to give demonstration rides struck her at "tremendous speed", according to witnesses—some 4 MPH (6.4 km/h). The driver had apparently modified the engine to allow the car to go faster.

The jury returned a verdict of "accidental death" after an inquest lasting some six hours. The coroner said: "This must never happen again." No prosecution was made.

While Bridget Driscoll was the first person killed by an automobile in the world, Henry Bliss (1831 to September 13, 1899) was the first person killed by an automobile in the United States. He was disembarking from a streetcar at West 74th Street and Central Park West in New York City, when an electric-powered taxicab (Automobile No. 43) struck him and crushed his head and chest. He died from these injuries the next morning.

The driver of the taxicab was arrested and charged with manslaughter but was acquitted on the grounds that it was unintentional.

So now I know. The Road acquired its taste for blood early. And Daddy Bliss and Road Mama have been parents to their family for a very long time.

My first really big assignment is coming up in a few days—the weekend of the OSU-Michigan football game. I've set up three different tracks for this. Thirty-eight fatalities and twenty injuries—not all in the same place, of course; the Road can't be *too* obvious about its methods.

I figured out a way to run several tracks simultaneously without blowing any fuses. I rig them to run off of car batteries. Seems to me there ought to be something ironic in there, but I'm too tired to figure it out.

I've been practicing with the controls. I've gotten really good. My hand/eye coordination has never been so sharp.

Ciera called me. Daddy Bliss is going to let her come visit me the weekend of the OSU-Michigan game. I'm really looking forward to seeing her. I remember the way she kissed me and hope she'll want to do it again. And maybe other stuff, too.

It's been a while.

And that's it. I don't know why I decided to write all of this down. Maybe to have some record, for my own sanity. Maybe I did it in case I decide to do a Miss Driscoll with some pudding and pills. But that would mean no Ciera weekend, so I doubt that's the reason. Hell, I don't know.

I tried to think of some clever way to end this, some witty remark that would leave you with a grin or something, and I'd almost decided on "Drive safely" but the truth is, even if you do—drive safely, that is—it won't make a damned bit of difference.

It never did. And never will.

Keep on truckin'....

(Special thanks to Geoff Cooper for sharing his near-encyclopedic knowledge of cars during the writing of this story.)

CONGESTION

(Thumpitty-thump-thump-thu...)

Had to do it yourself, didn't you? Had to bite the metaphorical bullet and drive yourself to the hospital. Had to ignore every goddamned warning the doctors have been issuing for the past year-and-a-half and do it your way, your way, your way or the highway.

Hey speaking of...isn't this a lovely traffic jam surrounding you? Cars to the left of you, cars to the right, cars up your ass and down your throat, nobody moving, nobody getting anywhere, and the exhaust fumes hanging around like vagrants outside a bus station on Friday night.

And let's not forget the air-conditioning in your own resplendent example of modern American automobile manufacturing. You remember, right? The air-conditioner that you should have gotten repaired a week ago but kept putting it off because, gosh-oh-golly-gee, you're a busy guy and, besides, it's—what?—mid-September, the official start of Fall only days away, so why bother with it now, it's not like any unexpectedly high temperatures are going to sneak up and surprise you, no, not here in God's own wonderful white-bread Midwest, that *never* happens, nosiree.

(Thumpitty-thump-thump-thu…)

So how come the back of your shirt is glued to the seat? Why do you suppose it is that you have to keep reaching up every fifteen seconds to wipe the sweat from your eyes? Oh, and there's also that steady trickle of perspiration that keeps sliding slowly, slowly, *slooooooowly* down the center of your middle-aged chest, pooling in the little grotto between your middle-aged man-boobs.

Yes, it happened—at age forty-mumble-mumble you've grown man-boobs; okay, maybe they're not particularly big or pendulous, but they're *boobs* nonetheless. You've seen enough boobs to know a pair on sight, and what you've got hanging there under your sweat-drenched shirt, those are definitely protuberances of the boob variety. Should have laid off the rich foods, pal; should have exercised more, or some, or *at all*, but this isn't really the time to point fingers, is it? No, not with the ninety-something degrees baking you inside and out, not with the traffic, not with the exhaust fumes that you have no choice but to breathe in because the only alternative is to roll up the windows and if you do that, the inside of this car becomes a crock pot in two minutes.

What to do, what to do?

You flip open the cell phone to check the charge. Full. Okay, so, you could call 911, tell 'em what's happening, but what good is that going to do? You think an ambulance is going to be able to get to you? Not through this congestion, not in this universe or any other where the laws of physics rule and rock. Sure, maybe there could be some divine intervention-type action and the cars would part like the Red Sea, but you probably shouldn't bet the farm on that one. Nope—the only way out is up, a Life-Flight helicopter, salvation from above.

Or you could get out and walk, hoof it to the exit and hope Ye Olde Ticker doesn't just *pop!* like a water balloon dropped from a high bridge.

You close the cell phone. The pain in your chest, it's ebbing. After three full nitro tablets, it damned well *ought* to be ebbing. Still—*Christ on a crutch*—why does it have to be this hot?

Pull in a breath, slowly, slow, there you go; now hold it, hold it, release slowly, just like that, good boy, control it, let it out, steady as she goes. Good. Think you can do it again? They say you can't live without love, but as far as you're concerned, oxygen might edge love out of the Number One slot, especially now—not that you'd turn down love were any to be offered, but this isn't a good time to get depressed about your romantic life; or, rather, the lack thereof. So breathe, just breathe, and wait it out.

(Thumpitty-thump-thump-thu...)

Man, it's that last one, that third, uncompleted *thump!* that gets you every time, isn't it? Not that it's ever actually *incomplete*—that would mean you're dead, in case you've forgotten—it's that epic *pause* between the *thu* and the *mp!* that throws a wrench into the works. That pause, it's been getting longer every time this happens. What was it this morning, something like seven seconds?

But you're a tough guy, you'll beat it, you can hold down the fort until this fucking traffic starts moving again because once that happens, the hospital exit is less than a mile away—hell, you can even see part of the sign up ahead. *Way* up ahead, sure, but you can see it, even through the haze of exhaust that's causing the whole world to shimmer and swirl and stink.

You put the cell phone on your lap and reach into your pocket for the bottle of nitro tablets. Just In Case. Just to have them in your hand. This doesn't mean you're giving up, doesn't mean you're admitting that you made a mistake by choosing to drive your own ass to the ER instead of doing what the doctors said, calling an ambulance so you could lay back and enjoy the ride; no, this is just a little insurance, a minor safety blanket like that *Peanuts* character—what's his name? *Linus!* Right. Just a safety blanket because Captain Action isn't around to protect you anymore.

Captain Action? Jeez-Louise…how long has it been since you thought of him? Probably the only human being walking the Earth today who remembers when Captain Action was *the* hero. Spider-Man, Superman, Batman, The Green Hornet? *Wimps* compared to Captain Action. Oh, how brightly and briefly his star did burn.

Okay, there it was, the *mp!* Better now. Keep up with the breathing and ignore the little lake of sweat between your man-boobs. Lean back your head, that's it, and let yourself melt a little.

Captain Action would never have allowed himself to grow man-boobs. You ought to be ashamed of yourself.

Had to do it, didn't you? Had to drive yourself to the hospital. Not a move that's going to make your Highlight Reel anytime soon, but what're you gonna do?

You're going to breathe slowly with the cell phone in your lap and the teeny bottle of nitro tablets in your hand. You're going to listen to the *Thumpitty-thump-thump-thump!* and make sure that third *thump!* doesn't make a pause for the cause.

Only now there's another sound, this one kind of…metallic.

Clatter-clatter-skit! Clatter-clatter-skit!

What the hell?

You turn and look out the window, blinking against the bright bursts of sunlight exploding from the chrome of the cars around and behind, and you try to make out whatever it is that's making that noise.

Clatter-clatter-skit! Clatter-clatter-skit!

And there it is, rolling toward you, rolling straight as you please right down the center of the lanes, moving with more purpose and speed than any vehicle here has been able to muster in the last fifteen minutes, rolling along like it doesn't have a care in the world, la-dee-dah, la-dee-dah.

A skate. Not a *roller-blade*—those have a line of wheels right down the middle; no, this is a *skate*, hard, firm, old-school, designed like a boot, two wheels in front, two in back, one of those rubber-stopper thingamajigs underneath the toe to use for a brake.

Clatter-clatter-skit! Clatter-clatter-skit!

You watch as the old-school skate comes rolling down toward your car, and you notice that there's something not quite right about it, something a bit off, off-*putting*, even, and it's not until the thing comes to a slow, squeaking stop right next to your car that you're able to pinpoint what's wrong.

There's still a foot inside of it. You know this because you can still see part of the bone sticking up from the dark glop of meat and blood marking the spot where the rest of the skater used to be attached. Okay; *this* might be Highlight Reel worthy, you admit.

(Thumpitty-thump-thump-thu…)

Oh, no—not gonna do this again. Huh-uh. No way.

(mp!)

Unscrewing the cap, you upend the nitro bottle and shake a tablet into your hand, raise the hand to your mouth, and slip the tablet under your tongue. Remembering to breathe slowly, natch.

All right, maybe there *isn't* a foot still inside the thing. Maybe your nerves have just gotten the better of you, along with the heat, the stink, your job, the lack of any special someone waiting for you at the end of the day, the price of gas, Ye Olde Ticker, the man-boobs, roaming charges, no rollover minutes, needing to piss, all of the above, none of the above, a potpourri of frustrations big and small, who knows, who cares, what's it matter in the bigger scheme of things, anyway when you can't just call on Captain Action to speed in and save the day?

So take a second look, make sure.

You wait until the tablet finishes dissolving and that cool rush envelopes your skull, then you lean out the window for another gander. Nope, had it right the first time; that's definitely a foot in there.

You close your eyes and lean forward, peeling your shirt from the seat and feeling Man-Boob Lake spill farther down your torso. You grip the steering wheel and place your forehead against the backs of your hands and close your eyes, fighting back the mild nausea that always hits you after a nitro tablet, only now it's compounded by the memory—not to mention the *smell*—of what's parked outside next to your door.

Think about

(Thumpitty-thump-thump-thu…)

something else, fer chrissakes. C'mon, it's not like your mind is a blank slate or anything, you're a busy guy, a lot on the plate, things to see, people to do…wait, scratch that…things to do, people to see…that's right, there you

(mp!)

go. Easy now, easy, easy, in, out, in, out, rolling your head back and forth, feeling the sweat squishing between your skull and hands.

Out there in the immobile sea of cars, somebody hits their horn. It sounds like an elephant fart. Some other car responds with a goose honk. A semi puts a stop to the conversation with a prolonged rhino belch.

God, you'd forgotten how much you *hate* cars, hate driving, hate it every time you have to climb into this future scrap heap and risk life and limb just to get from point A to point B and back again, all the while sputtering exhaust into the air, doing your part to help widen that hole in the ozone so people can have a nice surprise from time to time, like a hurricane, or tidal wave, or even a ninety-something-degree day in the middle of September with Fall only days away.

Inside a car parked in the next lane, a couple of kids start squealing. You roll your head to the right and open your eyes. Both kids have their faces pressed up against the windows, flattening out their cheeks. Mommy and Daddy have a car with air-conditioning that works, good for them.

"*Lookit the skate!*" the kids squeal. "*Lookit the skate! Lookit the skate!*" Bouncing up and down like it's the most funniest, really excitingest thing they've ever seen. Mommy and Daddy are in the front seat, arguing about something, paying no attention. You want to step on all of them, grind them under your heel.

Okay, maybe not. Mostly, you just want the kids to shut up. Want the traffic to start moving. Want a cloud to crawl across the face of the sun. Want a body that works like a body is supposed to, not betray you in a series of sputtering little agonies once you turn forty-mumble-mumble.

The car behind you sounds its horn, startling you. You snap upright and glare into the rear-view mirror. It's a fucking Isuzu. *Isuzu*—sounds like the name of some lesser god the Aztecs might have made sacrifices to. Guy driving it looks like a smug fucker, doesn't he? Like all of this was designed just to inconvenience *him*. Boo-hoo-hoo. The golf course will still be there in half an hour, douchebag, so why not get on your camera-phone with wireless Internet and download some manners?

(Thumpitty-thump-thump-thu…)

Please, no.

(mp!)

Good. You're not going to do it, not going to die stuck in traffic.

You flip open your cell phone once again and check the time. Twenty minutes now and nothing's moved but the skate.

"Lookit the skate!" squeal the kiddies next door, this time both of them pounding on the windows to get your attention. *"Lookit the skate!"*

So you look at the skate. Some of blood that's pulled atop the meat glop has begun trickling over the rim, spattering down onto the road. A thin rivulet of the stuff is snaking toward your left front tire.

And you remember why it is that you hate cars so much. You were seven years old. The family was driving back from the State

Fair, had just gotten off the exit, in fact, home less than ten minutes away. Dad was bitching about this guy on a motorcycle who'd been riding your tail for the last five minutes, and Mom, bless her, she was trying to calm him down, telling him to let it go, it had been such a *nice* day, why let some fool on a Harley ruin it for everyone. Then she turned around and smiled at you, sitting there in the back seat with the grandest single item you'd ever had in your possession, your *prize*, the item against which all other prizes won would be measured and come up lacking, the Holy Grail of All Things Cool, a stuffed Captain Action almost as big as you were. You'd won it at one of the game booths, tossing rings over the tops of milk bottles. Nobody thought you had a chance, but you'd done it, you'd *won*, and won big, your heart filled with so much pride and happiness you thought it was going to burst right out of your chest, the happiest day of your kid life. You smiled back at Mom and said, "Captain Action will make him go away!" And your Mom laughed, then Dad looked back, quickly, and said, "That's all right—you tell Captain Action it's the thought that counts." You giggled, then sat up and turned Captain Action around so that he was pointing his silver ray gun out the back window, and you said, "Zap*ow!*" because you always figured that was the sound Captain Action's ray gun made when he fired it at the aliens and bad guys and henchmen, *Zapow!* was a sound that told everybody this was serious business, it was time to surrender or prepare to meet your maker (even though, so far as you knew, Captain Action had never killed an enemy, only wounded them because heroes worked that way, they Only Wounded), so it was *"Zapow!"* a third time, and that's when the guy on the motorcycle swerved to the left and zoomed ahead of you, flipping up his middle finger at Dad as he sped by, not looking ahead toward the intersection, which was kinda dumb because how could you tell what might be coming around the corner if you didn't look (especially when you were going as fast as the guy on the motorcycle), but you *did* look, and you saw the big semi making the wide, wide, *wiiiiiide* turn before anyone else, even Dad, and you opened your mouth to say something but Mom, bless her, she'd seen it, too, and she gripped Dad's arm and said, *"Look out, Henry!"* and Dad hit the brakes and the car squealed as it slammed to a stop and that's when the guy on the motorcycle decided to turn and look in front of him but by then it was too late; he hit the front of the semi and his motorcycle went one way and he went another and something flew off and bounced against the road, bounced once, and then came slamming down on the hood of the car, causing Mom to scream and Dad to shout "Don't look! Don't look!" but you'd already looked, already seen the metallic-blue helmet skid right up to the windshield and it might have been funny except for the wet streak it painted right up the middle of the hood and the way the visor had been ripped off so you had a nice clear view of the guy's head still inside of it, and you wondered why it was that the helmet and head weren't stopping…

…it was two days later, in the hospital, Mom sitting beside your bed and crying, parts of her face bruised, other parts bandaged, that you listened to a doctor explain how it was that, sometimes, a person in the middle of experiencing a wreck will see everything happening like it was in slow-motion. "The mind can produce its own kind of trauma to protect you during times of physical trauma," the doctor had said. You didn't quite understand some of the words he used, but Mom, bless her, would stop him and translate for you just to make sure you understood. The helmet and head, they hadn't been slow at all; they'd flown back toward the car so fast and hard that they'd smashed right through the windshield. "If your daddy hadn't pushed me down," said Mom, "I might have been killed."

Captain Action had been destroyed when the helmet shot through the back windshield, taking off his head, as well.

It had only taken half of Dad's head…and even with that, most of it wound up splattered over your clothes. It had glanced off your shoulder on its way by, snapping part of your collarbone. You spent almost a week in the hospital. Mom held off having Dad's funeral until you were released.

Standing there by his grave, waiting for the priest to finish saying the final prayers, that's when you decided that cars and trucks and motorcycles were your sworn enemies, that you hated them, that they were evil and mean and ugly and nasty and horrible and you'd never ever-ever-*ever* get in another car for as long as you lived. (Even then you knew it was a silly vow to make because, after all, you'd ridden to the *funeral* in a car, and would have to ride back in the same car, only to get out of it and climb into Aunt Eunice's car because she'd given you and Mom a ride to the church, but you needed to swear something because Dad was down there, he was dead with only half his head, and it had been such a *nice* day for everyone, too….)

It was nearly a full year before you could ride in a car without cowering in fear every time another vehicle sped past on the other side of the road, blinking, wincing, holding your breath, your stomach in knots as you waited for the sound of shattering safety glass and the scream of twisting metal and the hot spatter of fresh blood to cover your face.

"Lookit the skate!"

You snap up your head—when had you rested it against the steering wheel again?—and look out once again.

The mind can produce its own kind of trauma to protect you during times of physical trauma.

But this isn't your mind playing any trauma-tricks on you. That skate is real, it is there, just like the remnants of the foot inside of it.

Fucking cars. Instruments of death, all of them. *Why* did you ever give into the pressure to get a license? You'd been perfectly happy, taking the bus or—God forbid!—*walking* places. But if a man were going to be a success in this world, he had to have his wheels, and not just a good, solid, dependable set of unadorned commonplace wheels, oh, no—a man had to have a *snazzy* car, an *expensive* car, a car that would make other cars envious because it made them aware of their own inferiority, their shortcomings, their motorized mediocrity.

(Thumpitty-thump-thump-thu…)

Please, no.

(mp!)

So you bought into it, didn't you? That whole "He Who Dies With The Best Toys Wins" mentality that everyone *said* went out of fashion in the Eighties but in reality only dressed itself up in more conservative clothing and Machiavellian language; people weren't "fired" anymore, they were *outsourced.* Call it whatever you wanted to, it all boiled down to the same thing: the rich got richer, the poor got poorer, and the in-betweens, they killed themselves on a day-to-day basis just to keep running in place. The 'tweens, they got the high blood pressure, the irritable bowel syndrome, the angina. The 'tweens found themselves never judging those who were richer or poorer than they were because, well, hell, they had no idea in which direction they were headed themselves, so it wouldn't do to make enemies on either side of the economic scale and

(Thumpitty-thump-thump-thu...)

Please, no.

(mp!)

Calm down. You need to calm down. So you do the cell-phone flip once more. Twenty-five minutes. It feels like you've been stuck in here all day. Damn good thing you filled up the tank last night. Still, there was no telling how much longer you might be stuck here, so maybe you ought to just shut it off for a while, until things started moving again...of course, with your luck, the second you turned off the engine, whatever was causing this congestion would magically disappear and all the cars would start lurching ahead and you'd turn the key and the damn car would stall out, you know it, so you'll just let it idle for a while longer, see what happens.

Your clothes are drooping on your body, soaked in sweat. The kids over there are still bouncing and squealing and pointing. And the Isuzu behind you is smiling.

What the—?

The mind can produce its own kind of trauma to protect you during times of physical trauma.

Goddamn thing *is* smiling, you can see it. The metal of its front is starting to curl upward at the edges. You can hear the low *screeeech* of everything twisting itself into place. Looks like the goddamned Cheshire Cat.

You glance at the kids next door to see if they've noticed, but they're still entranced by the skate. The trail of blood slithering from beneath its wheels has grown thicker, more defined, forming a straight red line from the skate to your car, almost like an arrow.

The Isuzu has a wide, shit-eating smile. One if its headlights winks at you. The Ford Gargantua—or whatever the hell kind of urban tank that is—parked in the lane next to Smiley is starting to giggle, its grille shaking, headlights narrowing as it tries to hold it in, but it can't anymore, and lets fly with a laugh and a smile, and now both it and Smiley are bouncing up and down, just like the kids, and chuckling it up, and a couple of horns sound again—a belch and a sneeze—before a few other cars start chortling, mocking you.

You're so upset by being laughed at that it takes a moment for you to notice that a cloud has floated across the face of the sun, casting shadows—

Thumpitty-thump-thump-thu…

—no, hold on, not shadows—

The mind can produce its own kind of trauma to protect you during times of physical trauma

—it's gotten *dark*. Jesus H! It's *night*! When did this happen?

Shaking your head, you fumble your hand up over your head, fingers searching for the interior light. You find it, switch it on, filling the car with a dull glow.

Outside, visibar lights from several emergency vehicles strobe all around. Radios crackle with buzzed conversation. A bright light shines down toward the ground just outside your door.

And half of Dad's head is lying on the passenger seat.

"You know," he says to you, "it didn't even *hurt*. Seems like something that takes off half your skull should at least *smart* a little."

"Says you," replies the head of the guy on the motorcycle, still stuck inside the metallic-blue helmet that's now balanced on your dashboard. "At least you died instantly. Did you know that a decapitated human head can still *see* for thirty seconds? No shit—it takes the brain that long to figure out what's happened and then shut down. Why do you think that during the French Revolution they always held up the heads of prisoners who'd just been guillotined? It wasn't just so the crowd could cheer, it was so the person had enough time to look down, see their body, and think, 'Huh. I'm dead.' Then they were."

"Thirty seconds?" asks Dad.

"Yeah. After I bounced off Junior's shoulder and went through the rear windshield, the momentum spun me around. I got to see my body laying there in the middle of the road and twitching."

You look in the rear-view mirror and see Captain Action sitting back there, his silver ray gun pointed at the back of your head.

"Zapow?" he says.

You nod.

"Had to try and drive yourself to the hospital, didn't you?" asks Dad.

You look at the bottle of nitro tablets in your hand.

"Don't feel too bad," Dad says, giving half a smile (since he's only got half a head, it makes sense); "I'd've probably done the same thing."

"We getting this show on the road, or what?" asks Harley Head.

You clear your throat. "I, uh…how long have I—?"

"About an hour," says Dad.

"Ah." You look out at the skate, spotlighted now as police photographers move in slow half-circles around it, snapping away, getting photos from every angle.

Someone knocks on the rear passenger-side window. You turn around as the kid opens the door and does not so much *slide* into the back seat as fall. He's wearing a helmet, elbow- and knee-pads, and one skate on his right foot; at the end of his left leg, a bloody stump is still spattering a little blood. The kid's really pale. Makes sense. You lose that much blood, your skin's going to show it.

"Glad I caught you," he says. "I tried to, y'know, *skate* the rest of the way, but my balance is shot to hell. I think I busted something inside one of my ears when I hit the pavement." He closes the door. "You don't mind me catching a lift, do you?"

You shake your head. "Not at all."

Harley Head asks, "Did it hurt much?"

The kid laughs. "Y'know, it *did*. Not for long, though."

You point outside. "You want me to…maybe get out and—?"

The kid shakes his head. "Don't really need it anymore. But thanks."

You put the car in **Drive** and pull away. After a few seconds, you look into the rear-view mirror and see yourself sitting back there in your car, your head flopped against the headrest, eyes open wide and staring.

"Anybody know where we're headed?" asks the skater.

No one does. But that's okay. You've got plenty of gas. Maybe you'll take the scenic route, see what there is to see.

merge
RIGHT

Before realizing that he was screwed to the wall, that he was beyond merely *lost*, that somewhere between 8:45 and 11:00 p.m. the universe as he knew it (or *thought* he'd known it) had ceased to function under anything even remotely resembling the acknowledged laws of physics, Matt Leigh ventured outside one winter evening, set the urn containing his wife's ashes on the passenger seat of his car, buckled it in place, took a mental snapshot of the home he had shared with her, and drove off to fulfill her last request.

Scatter my ashes at Niagara Falls in winter.

Part of him cursed himself for ever having decided to do it—God, how *lame* could you be?—and then just as quickly realized that Lauren had *liked* lame, had always been something of a traditional romantic at heart (one of the things he'd always loved about her; after all, they'd honeymooned at Niagara Falls), and considering how miserable the last few weeks of her life had been, it would have been a betrayal to her memory to do otherwise.

As he merged onto I-71 and headed toward Cleveland, he glanced over at the urn, felt the sudden tightness in his chest that always preceded a crying jag, and swore that this time he wouldn't allow it to get the upper hand; there had been too many times in the past few months that he'd broken into tears before he was even aware of it, the people around him lapsing into an uncomfortable silence, unable to maintain eye contact because he was blubbering like an idiot. The public breakdowns were bad enough, sure, but the solitary ones were even worse, somehow more embarrassing, because he felt defeated, frightened, alone, and—worst of all—*weak*. Christ, when he lost it at that memorial service they'd held for Lauren at the high school where she'd taught Science, he thought he'd implode from the humiliation.

There might have been a time, once, not so long ago, when he was a different sort of man, a kinder man, a man of compassion and selflessness who did not feel at all embarrassed or self-conscious about letting his feelings show, about wearing his heart on his sleeve, but then came the baby that was too sick to live and Lauren fell in on herself after the funeral and said almost nothing for a full month until one night she surprised him with a tight hug and a deep kiss and a "I'm going to treat myself to a long, quiet bubble bath," and she did, and that's where he found her a little over an hour later, the remaining foam stained to a sick-making shade of pink, the water a distilled red, her face so calm, so relaxed, so peaceful. Her note, taped to the bathroom mirror, had for the most part been brief and to the point: *I'm sorry, Matt. I hope you'll forgive me. I love you. Scatter my ashes at Niagara Falls in winter.*

This, followed by something that he hadn't understood at all: *All matter is composed of quarks and leptons.* Written in a different color of ink.

He assumed that she'd written the note on a piece of paper that she'd used to scribble some notes for class. That would be just like her—never waste anything if you can find another way to use it.

Later, he confessed to one of his friends that he'd been suspicious—no, he'd *known* she was going to do it, and did nothing to stop her. "She was so unhappy," he said. "And nothing was going to make it any better for her. I tried, I really did, but nothing I did or said got through to her."

"Bullshit," said his friend. "You're just trying to find a way to blame yourself for being the one who's still alive."

Maybe that was right. Maybe. But Matt had spent so much time looking into himself since Lauren's death that he didn't know what to think or believe. There were times he thought some part of him was *relieved* that she'd done it. God, how many times had Lauren told him (in those rare instances when they had a conversation lasting more than a minute) that she couldn't look at him because the sight of him was just another reminder of what they'd lost? He could never bring himself to admit to Lauren that he felt the same way whenever he looked at her, and hated himself for it.

It's too soon, he told himself now. *She's only been gone a few months, it's too soon to do this. Turn around, go back home, and wait until next winter. Keep her around a little longer.*

He reached up and wiped his eyes, then pulled in a hard, loud, snot-filled breath.

Jesus Christ, babe—why? Why'd you do it? We could have gotten through it. I would have done anything *to make it better for you, I was just too wrapped up in feeling sorry for myself to notice how much more you were hurting. I loved you* so much. *So much. Do you have any idea how much I miss you?*

If he turned around right now, he could be back home in half an hour. The weather report called for another inch or two of snow tonight, and New York was supposed to get twice that much. Okay, sure, he'd known this before, but had decided he'd rather try braving the snow at night rather than have to deal with both the snow *and* traffic. Six hours from start to finish, one way; seven if he took it slowly.

He checked his watch. Not quite 6:30 p.m. The plan was to leave at 6:00 and get into Niagara Falls a little after midnight. He'd booked the hotel room a week ago. He'd get up in the morning, have breakfast, check out, and then walk across the Rainbow Bridge, where he'd scatter her ashes. Matt wasn't sure if it was legal or not, and didn't really care. So what if he had to pay a fine?

You could have checked, he thought. *Another reason to turn around. What the hell good is any of this going to be if you get there and find out it's against the law?*

He shook his head. It wouldn't make any difference. He was just trying to find a way to chicken out.

He looked at the urn once more and said, "Don't worry, babe. I won't let you down, I promise. I just…I can't stop thinking about how *miserable* you must have been, y'know?"

And then he heard Lauren's voice in his head, saying to him the thing she always said whenever his mood turned dark: *You need to think about something funny, Mr. Grumpy-Pants. You need to think about something that will make you smile.*

"Easy for you to say," Matt whispered. "You're not the one who's been left to sift through the detritus. You're not the one who's been left with a list of unanswered questions longer than your arm. You're not the one who..." He bit down on his lip, stopping himself. To say it out loud would be to give it form, to move it from the world of one's private thoughts into the physical world. Okay, okay, maybe that was a bit existential, but nonetheless, Matt feared that if he said it, if he gave it voice, if he spoke the words, then the terrible thought in his head would always be out here in the world, following him, reminding him that there was a time when he'd told the universe that, despite his claims of relief, he still felt as if his wife had *abandoned* him, had lied to him somehow, and that some part of him *hated* her for it. As long as the thought remained in his head and *only* in his head, then it was safe...safe enough. It was something he could push back, file away, learn to ignore. But once *spoken....*

Deciding that he needed a distraction, Matt flipped down the visor and selected a compact disc from the sleeve mounted on the back, slid it into the player, and adjusted the volume. The disc was one he'd made for Lauren for their last anniversary, a compilation of her favorite Peter Gabriel songs. Though Matt personally preferred the stuff Gabriel had done with Genesis back in the day, he'd come around to appreciating the solo material, thanks to Lauren (although "Shock the Monkey" still got on his nerves no end). He'd promised himself that he'd play this for her along the way.

The disc opened with a live version of "In Your Eyes"—the version Lauren preferred—and Matt found himself humming along. Somehow the song seemed to fit the night outside because it was the perfect contrast; where the song was rich, deep, and warm, the night was bleak, impenetrable, and so very cold. The music, it seemed, was protecting them both from the elements.

He double checked to make sure his cell phone was charging, flipped the visor back into place, and opened a can of Pepsi he'd taken from the small cooler on the passenger-side floor; he'd stocked the thing with sodas, a couple of sandwiches, and some snacks before leaving; this way he'd only have to stop to use the bathroom. The car had a full tank (and had always gotten damned good highway mileage, even in bad weather when he had to drive at a crawl), so he wouldn't have to gas up until it was time to start the trip home.

Somehow he was able to let himself slip into auto-pilot for a little while, becoming just another weary driver out on the road, moving, moving, moving along. Sometimes this was the best way to do things; just take most of your conscious self out of it and let your body function by rote.

He merged onto I-271 N via exit 220 toward Erie, Pennsylvania just as it became fully dark and the predicted snow was beginning to fall. This was really, truly, sincerely *it*—Put-Up or Shut-Up time. A little over a hundred miles into the trip. This was his last chance to turn around if he were going to do it.

"What do you think, babe?" he asked the urn. "Keep going or go home?"

He looked at the urn as if he actually expected it to respond, and then realized this was the *second* time he'd spoken to it. That couldn't be a good sign.

Okay, he thought to himself. *If you keep her*—it, *if you keep* it *around another year, how sure are you that you're not going to* continue *talking to it like it's really her?*

"Good point," he said to the urn. "Onward we go, then."

A few miles after getting onto I-271 he saw the sign telling him to **Merge Right**. So he did, noting that what had been a four-lane stretch was now only three. He glanced out over the concrete divider but saw no other cars traveling in the opposite direction, which seemed odd; it wasn't quite 8:00 p.m. yet, there should still have been a decent amount of traffic on the road.

Unless the forecast changed and they're calling for a lot more snow than was originally expected. Four or five inches would keep everyone home.

Up ahead, a gray car sat in the emergency lane, its taillights flashing, exhaust billowing into the winter night, sketching odd shapes into the air. Matt wondered if he should pull over and see if the driver needed help—were Lauren still here, *she'd* have pulled over—but then realized that it was exactly under circumstances like these that many serial killers had snatched their victims; no wonder so many people were now wary of a long stretch of dark, semi-empty road. Sure, odds were this was no serial killer, but that's probably what all the *victims* thought when they made the decision to pull over and play Good Samaritan. Didn't those two guys…what were their names?—Henry Lee Lucas and Ottis Toole, right—didn't they claim to have gotten a lot of their victims that way, by faking car trouble in hopes that some poor, unsuspecting Samaritan-type would pull over and offer to lend a hand?

Despite this line of thinking, Matt found himself slowing down as he neared the stopped car. He leaned forward, head turned toward the other vehicle, and tried to get a look inside. The dome light was off, but the illumination from the dashboard cast a soft bluish glow over the interior, and as far as Matt could see, there was no one inside the car.

He pulled a bit farther ahead and saw that the windshield wipers weren't going, so getting a better look inside from this angle was out of the question. God Almighty, why was he even doing this? He could see the exhaust, the lights of the dashboard, the flashing taillights, it wasn't like the car wasn't working, so how much of an emergency could it be? Maybe the driver just needed to pull over and check the map, or make a call on their cell phone, or even—hey, *here's* one that should have been obvious—run off into the bushes to take a leak. Matt could sympathize. There had been a few occasions where he'd thought he could make it to the next rest stop, only to find that his bladder had just been messing with him, had just been waiting for the moment when the previous rest stop was no longer visible in the rear-view mirror before announcing that, yep, okay, *now* it's time to go with the flow.

He began to pull away when, once again, something made him hesitate. *What* the hell was wrong with him? The driver was just down there in the trees somewhere, writing his name in the snow.

But what if you're wrong? said Lauren's voice in his head. *What if he pulled over because he was having a heart attack or a seizure or an asthma attack or something? What if he's inside, lying across the seat and dying? What if he can't reach his cell phone? What if he doesn't even* have *one?*

Matt glared at the urn for a few moments, then looked at the other car once again. *Three minutes*, he thought, checking his watch. *I'll give this guy three minutes, and then it's none of my business.* This seemed practical. The car had been idling here well before Matt spotted it, so waiting an additional three minutes would give the guy *plenty* of time to finish his business, even if he had to do more than take a leak.

"You're stalling," he said aloud to himself. "And you know it. The guy's fine."

Hell, the guy was probably down there *hiding* in the bushes at this point, wondering what the person in the other car wanted. The thought brought the week's first genuine smile to Matt's face. He put himself in the other guy's position: it's dark, and he has to pull over to relieve himself, so he sprints down into the bushes to do his business, and when he's finishing up, lo and behold, another car has pulled up alongside his and isn't moving. *Anyone* could be in that car—the police, car thieves, or a pair of sickos who idolize Henry and Otis. *No way* is he going anywhere *near* his car until the other vehicle is long gone.

Matt almost laughed, then thought of the poor guy down there freezing his nuts off—perhaps literally—and so sped up and drove away, quietly wishing the other fellow the best of luck.

With the exception of the snow—which swirled across the windshield like heavy smoke from a distant fire—the next forty minutes of the drive were smooth and uneventful, if a bit slow due to decreased visibility. Then Matt saw another sign instructing him to **Merge Right** slip into the glow of his headlights, and he did so, and the three-lane stretch of highway became two. Once again—a force of habit, he supposed—he glanced over the concrete divider and saw there was still no traffic heading in the opposite direction, and that's when it occurred to him that he couldn't remember seeing *any* other cars (aside from the empty one in the emergency lane way back there) since the last time he'd merged.

Maybe the rest of the world was staying in tonight. That was fine with Matt, were it the case. Just him and Lauren and the road all to themselves.

Okay, that's the third time you've done something like, thought of the urn as her and not a thing, an object. Knock it off.

He looked at the urn, reached out to touch her—*it*, reached out to touch *it*—pulled his hand back at the last moment, and then touched it, anyway.

"Why didn't you talk to me about how you were feeling?" he whispered. "I would've listened. Why didn't you…?"

He stopped himself from finishing the question. Who was here to answer?

Then, two more signs: the first said **Roadside Emergency, Dial *891.**

The second: **Merge Right**.

What the—? Why did he need to merge again so soon? Now it was down to one lane on his side.

Checking the rear-view mirror to make sure no one was behind him, Matt pulled off onto the emergency lane, put the car in park, removed the TripTik from the driver's-side door pocket, and leaned down for a better look at the map. Maybe he'd let himself drift off a little too much and had missed an exit or something…but, no, according to the map, he was right on track, and wouldn't hit any construction for at least another hundred miles.

He looked up into the rear-view mirror once again. There was still no one behind him. How long ago had he passed that car? Forty, forty-five minutes, right? And he hadn't passed any exits since then, so where was the other guy? Matt had driven enough road trips to know that, for a while, anyway, you tended to share your side of the highway with the same group of cars; not only had he *not* seen any other vehicles, but the guy that he passed back there should have caught up with him by now.

Oh, Jesus, he thought. *What if the guy really* was *hurt, or sick, or having a heart attack? What if he really was lying across the front seat and* that's *why you didn't see him?*

Folding the map back into place, he unplugged his cell phone, checked for the signal, and dialed *891. At least he knew where he was, and how far back the other guy had been.

There was a single ring on the other end, followed by a *click!*, and then…nothing. Just white noise, a soft static hiss that Matt imagined would be the voice of snow, if snow had a voice. He closed the phone, said, "Shit!", and then opened it again and hit the "redial" button. This time it rang three times before the *click!* And white noise came in, and just as he was about to close the phone again, a voice came on and said, "If tin whistles are made of tin, then what do they make foghorns out of?"

"What?" said Matt. "Who the hell is this? Listen, I've got an emergency I need to report. I'm on I-271, about—"

"—the only way to get home is never to stop. Never to stop. Never to—"

Matt snapped closed the phone and tossed it onto the dashboard. Screw this; he'd get off at the next exit, find a service station, and get his bearings once again. According to the TripTik, there was an exit less than four miles ahead. Hopefully the service station would have a CB or something, or a phone that worked.

He put the car in gear and pulled back out onto the highway. "Jesus Christ, baby!" he said to the urn. "I try to call for help and what do I get? 'Weirdoes 'R' Us! I should've listened to you, baby, I'm sorry."

By now the snowfall was fairly steady; combined with the light wind, it looked as if he were driving on a sheet of slowly roiling fog.

"We're fine, baby," he said to the urn, not looking at it. "We'll get you there, no worries. We just gotta make an extra stop, that's all. Get that guy some help." He tightened his grip on the steering wheel and leaned slightly forward, though why leaning forward would do anything to help visibility, he couldn't say. He'd always done this when driving in bad weather. If nothing else, it lessened the distance between his skull and the windshield should anything happen.

Damn cheerful fellow you are.

Merge Right.

"Fuck!" he made a fist and hit the steering wheel. Less than half a mile since the last one, and still not an orange construction barrel in sight.

He merged, and the concrete divider came closer to his side.

"Sorry, baby," he said. "I didn't mean to swear like that. I know how you hate it."

Three miles until the exit. No problem. He'd maintain, he *had* to maintain, he wanted to do this right, wanted to go to sleep later tonight knowing that he'd done the right thing, that he'd helped another human being before it was too late *and* honored his wife's last request. Maybe that would make it easier for him to sleep nights, easier to get up in the morning and face himself.

Two miles to go. He relaxed his grip on the steering wheel and even put in a new CD—Pat Metheny this time. Somehow, Metheny's guitar playing always sounded joyous, and he needed to hear something joyous and optimistic right now. Damn, had his nerves gotten the better of him—and a lot sooner than he'd thought they would.

One mile to go, and he saw the blinking taillights in the emergency lane ahead. This time he *would* stop, if for no other reason than to see if the other driver was as confused by all the **Merge Right** signs as he was.

And to make sure he's all right, said Lauren's voice. *To check and make sure he's okay. Like you should have done when you realized how long I'd been up in the tub.*

He looked at the urn. "That's a lousy thing to say to me, baby. I always respected your privacy, y'know? I just thought—"

No, honey, you just knew, *that's all. You knew, and you just* sat *there.*

"I'm sorry," he said, a single tear slipping from his eye and streaming slowly down his face. "I'm sorry, I'm sorry, *I'm so sorry!*"

This time it was an SUV of some sort, and the windshield wipers were going so Matt had a decent view of the inside, but no sooner had he come to a stop alongside the other vehicle than the wind kicked into a higher gear and the snow became a churning mass of white, so it didn't matter if the other vehicle's wipers were going; the wet snow plastered itself against the passenger windows of Matt's car and blocked his vision as much as did the tears.

He pressed his hands against his eyes and rubbed hard, pulling in his breath to steady himself. Get a grip, pal; just get a fucking grip already.

He looked over at the SUV, and then pulled back a bit and blinked his lights, hoping the other driver would see and blink his in return; when that didn't happen, Matt hit his horn three times. The driver of the SUV did the same. Matt didn't want to approach the other vehicle without having given the driver some sort of warning.

Reaching into the back seat, Matt retrieved his coat and put it on, zipping up and covering his head with the hood. He dug out his gloves, put those on, took a deep breath, said, "I'll be back in a minute, baby," and climbed out.

The weather reports had called for a low of 27 degrees, but what Matt stepped out into felt damned near arctic. It was so cold that his breath turned to iron in his throat, the hairs in his nostrils webbed into instant ice, and his eyes watered and stung. In the faint starlight and bluish luminescence of the snow, everything beyond a few yards of his gaze swam deceptive and without depth, glimmering with things half seen or imagined. He listened beneath the low, mournful call of the winter-night wind and could detect no sounds save for those made by himself, the purring motors of the two vehicles, and the *thunka-thunka-thunk* of windshield wipers. Everything else in the world might have died out there in the cold.

He raised a hand to wave in greeting as he approached the driver's-side of the SUV and realized that the driver had already lowered the window. Matt walked up to the door and offered his hand.

The SUV was empty. Not only that, but the window had been down for quite some time; a thin layer of snow covered a good portion of the front seats and part of the back. Despite the cold, the heater wasn't running, and appeared not have been running for quite some time; the snow had frozen into clumps in places.

Matt opened the door and leaned in, looking into the back seat where he saw a blanketed infant's seat buckled into place. Scrambling inside, he reached back and pulled away the blanket to find that the infant's seat was empty, as well. Jesus Christ—what kind of a moron would take a *baby* out into a night like this, especially when his or her car wasn't in good working order? The taking-a-leak scenario didn't hold up this time, because no one would leave a baby alone in a car on a night like this, regardless of how much they needed to go. Which meant that this person—whoever they were—was out there someplace with a baby.

Matt took a deep breath, feeling the cold slice into his throat, and tried to get a handle on the panic he felt rising in his gut. Okay, maybe they'd had some kind of car trouble—like the heater going out—and they'd decided that, rather than risk the baby's health, they'd call AAA Roadside Assistance and get a ride into the next town. But why leave the vehicle running like this? Dammit, dammit, *dammit*—this made no sense.

He looked around the interior of the car for anything that might be a clue, checking the door pockets, under the visors, even opening the glove compartment, but found nothing to indicate why they'd left the vehicle—or, for that matter, who "they" even were. The glove compartment held no registration papers.

Then he saw the three square buttons over the driver's visor: a GPS system. Sliding into the driver's seat and closing the door, Matt then raised the window and pressed the button with the imprinted phone icon.

After a few seconds, a voice said, "UniStar, how may I assist you?"

"Thank God," said Matt. "Listen, this isn't my car, I found it abandoned a few minutes ago. Whoever was driving this took a baby with them and it's snowing like crazy outside and—"

"One moment please while I confirm your location."

The next five seconds seemed like fifty, but at last the voice came back: "You say you found the car abandoned?"

"Yes."

"We have a fix on your location, Mr. Leigh, and will—"

"Hold on a second."

"Yes, Mr. Leigh?"

"How do you know my name? I never told you what it was."

"I apologize, sir. It's something we do automatically. As soon as anyone calls in, their name, vehicle make, and location shows on the screen. I was just reading the name off the screen. Force of habit."

"That still doesn't answer my question."

"Sir, the vehicle that you found is registered to a Matthew and Lauren Leigh."

Matt stared at the button, then looked out at his own car. "Lady, there must be some kind of mistake. *I'm* Matthew Leigh, and I can assure you I've *never* owned an SUV."

"Perhaps your wife—"

"My wife is dead. She's *been* dead for several months."

"Perhaps this is just one of those odd coincidences you hear about from time to time, Mr. Leigh. Perhaps the owners of this vehicle just happen to have the same names and yourself and your late wife."

Matt didn't like the flippant tone in the voice. "That's not funny."

"I wasn't trying to be, Mr. Leigh. Regardless, we'll have assistance to your location shortly."

Matt looked at the baby seat in the back and knew that, despite this bullshit about the names, he couldn't just leave this vehicle if there were *any* possibility that he could do something to help find a missing infant. "How soon will someone be here?"

"Mr. Leigh?"

"*What?*"

"The only way to get home is never to stop. Never to stop. Never to—"

"*Who the hell are you?*"

There was no answer. He repeated the question twice more, and, receiving no reply, decided to wait it out in his own car. As he was climbing back out into the freezing night, the voice said, "Assistance will be there in five minutes." *Click.*

The wind seemed determined to nail him to the spot—God, the temperature must have dropped at least eight more degrees while he was in the SUV—but he managed to make it back.

"Miss me?" he asked the urn as he climbed inside and closed the door. Removing his gloves, he reached down and turned up the heat, then grabbed his cell phone. Screw UniStar and their promises of assistance and their…whatever-in-the-hell it was that helped them to identify him; he was going to call the police. Punching in **911** he listened for a moment, heard nothing, then pulled back the phone and looked at the screen. *No Available Signal.*

"Horseshit!" he snapped, closing the phone and slowing his breathing. "You can't drive a mile down any stretch of highway without passing a goddamn cell tower these days, and I'm supposed to believe that a little snowstorm kills the signal? I don't think so." He looked at Lauren's urn. "I mean, c'mon, baby—for what we pay for this service every month, I damned well *ought* to get a signal. Isn't that their guarantee? Christ, I'd settle for weirdoes again."

He flipped open the phone once again and thumbed in **911**. This time he got results.

"911. Please state the nature of your emergency."

"I found an abandoned vehicle with an empty baby seat in the back. I think the driver and the baby might be lost in the snow."

"What is your location, Mr. Leigh?"

Matt pulled the phone away and stared at the screen. Instead of displaying the time and the number he'd just called, the words **Voice Mail Waiting** were showing.

He brought the phone back and said, "How do you know my name? What the hell is going on?" His only answer was a burst of white noise from the other end. He disconnected the call and tossed down the phone, leaning back against the headrest and closing his eyes.

You're stressing, honey, said Lauren's voice.

"I know," he whispered. "But, Jesus, baby…this is weird."

No arguments here. Out of curiosity, how long had *I been up there before you thought something might be wrong?*

Matt opened his eyes and sat forward. The UniStar folks knew the location of the SUV and were sending assistance, so he'd done his good deed for the day. The 911 thing…okay, maybe he got one of those stations that automatically pulls up the cell number and the name of the person it's registered to, maybe that was it.

He checked the time and saw that he was over an hour behind schedule. Reaching into his coat pocket, he removed the slip of paper with the name and number of the hotel. He'd call and tell them he was running late, that they were to hold the room. If it turned out there were any extra charges for this, so be it. (Part of him knew this was unnecessary, that he'd given them a credit card number to guarantee the room, but another part of him, the part that always worried, the part that always assumed the worst was going to happen, wouldn't let him *not* call.)

He flipped open his cell phone and saw the **Voice Mail Waiting** message again, and so pressed **OK**, entered his password, and waited for the message to play.

"Sorry we're not going to make it by midnight, baby," he said to Lauren. "But we'll get there. You just relax."

"I'm not worried, honey," came Lauren's voice from the cell phone. "I know you'll get us there eventually. Just remember, the best way to get there is never to stop."

Everything inside Matt's body locked up. For a moment, there was nothing more to the world than the echo of his dead wife's voice.

"To replay this message," came the electronic voice-prompt, "press '1'. To save it, press '7'. To delete it, press '9'."

Matt pressed "1."

"It's really cold out here, Daddy," said a child's thin voice. "When you gonna get here for me an' Mommy?"

Matt dropped the phone as if it were a hot coal and pressed his back up against the driver's-side door, instinctively pulling his knees up and remembering something a Psych professor had said when he was in college, about how childhood and fear are forever connected in the mind, because even an adult, in the grip of fear, will resort to the fetal position.

On the floor, the cell phone's screen blinked at him as the child's voice kept speaking: "…at, Daddy? It's so cold here. You have to come get me an' Mommy. Please, Daddy?"

Matt pushed out one leg and closed the cell phone with his foot, then pulled his leg back so quickly he heard the bones in his knee crack.

A sudden bright light appeared in the rear-view mirror. Turning around in his seat (still keeping his knees pressed tightly against his chest), Matt saw the distant headlights closing in fast.

"Okay," he said, but whether it was to himself or to Lauren, he didn't know and didn't care; for the moment, he need the sound of his own voice to fill the silence.

Silence?

He looked down at the CD player; the Metheny album had been playing when he'd gotten out of the car and he hadn't stopped it.

I always hated Pat Metheny, said Lauren. *All his stuff sounds the same to me after a couple of songs.*

He leaned forward and saw the ejected disc, now snapped in two, lying on the floor in front of Lauren's seat. As he reached down to pick it up, to make sure it was real and not just something brought on by the stress, his cell phone began ringing. He pulled back so quickly that he slammed his elbow against the steering wheel, right smack dead-bang on the funny bone, and the pain shot both up and down his arm as he grabbed his elbow and bent his arm, crying out.

The headlights down the highway were getting much closer now, and his cell phone—which should have switched over to voicemail after the fourth ring—was still going off, insistent, its volume growing louder and louder. He bent down—taking care to keep his throbbing arm a good distance from the steering wheel—snatched the phone from the floor, looked back to see how close the other vehicle was, and answered.

"*What?*" he shouted.

"You're beyond the laws of nature, time, gravity, friction, all of it," said a voice that was a combination of Lauren's soft Southern lilt and the child's tiny whisper. It sounded almost computerized. "Picture two people standing apart from one another on a frozen lake. They're tossing a basketball back and forth between them. Each time one person receives the basketball, the force of the other's throw pushes them farther away along the ice. The two players are the matter particles which are being interacted with, and the basketball is the force-carrier particle which affects them. One important thing to know about force-carriers is that a particular force-carrier particle can only be absorbed or produced by a matter particle which is affected by that particular force. For instance, electrons and protons have an electric charge, so they can produce and absorb the electromagnetic force-carrier, the photon. Neutrinos, on the other hand, have no electric charge, so they cannot absorb or produce photons. Isn't that interesting? I wish I'd gotten to teach some of this to my students…not that they would have paid much attention."

"Why are you doing this, baby?" said Matt into the phone, bursting into tears once again and feeling diminished, inept, and so goddamned *weak* he just wanted to die.

"*Shhh*, honey, don't get upset," said the voice of his dead wife and child. "All matter, be it the car in which you're sitting or a meteor in space, is composed of quarks and leptons. Both quarks and leptons exist in three distinct sets. Each set of quark and lepton charge-types is called a "generation" of matter—charges +2/3, -1/3, 0, and -1 as you go down each generation. All visible matter in the universe is made from the first generation of matter particles—up quarks, down quarks, and electrons. This is because all second and third generation particles are unstable and quickly decay into stable first generation particles.

"Now, think about something, honey. Imagine that *we're*—little Cynthia and I—imagine that we're a first-generation quark and *you're* a first-generation lepton, and that your guilt, your grief—whatever you want to call it—imagine that it has become so powerful that it's engineered a specific first generation force-carrier which, upon interaction with the first generation quarks and leptons, scrambles them into an instantaneous decay pattern and reduces the object to a harmless spray of subparticles. Do you see?"

"Oh, God, no, *no, I don't!* What're you talking about, baby? *Where* are you?"

"Right beside you, honey. A bunch of particles in a jar. The Universe is no longer a great mystery, Matt. In fact"—and here she/they laughed—"it's kind of a bore. Everything was always a bore without you by my side to share it with. Even dying."

Click!

He had to get out. He suddenly didn't give a damn if he got to Niagara Falls or not, or whether or not he found some help for that other car stranded way back there, or if he ever saw another sunrise; all he cared about right now was getting away from the car and the urn and the phone and the guilt in his gut, all of it.

The headlights were almost here, so Matt tossed down the still-active phone, flipped up the hood of his coat, threw open the door, and stepped outside—

—and no sooner was his first leg out of the car with the rest of his body automatically following that he immediately felt himself *drop* with such suddenness and force that he barely had to time to think *The ground's disappeared* before his arms were flailing out, hands seeking purchase, and he somehow managed to grab hold of the seat belt that pulled out to its farthest length and then locked in place as he *hung* there, his head at the level of the running board, gripping the seat belt, swinging back and forth, the rest of his body hanging over an endless, seemingly bottomless, black, black, *black* chasm. He pulled up his free arm and threw it over the running board, trying to grab onto the gearshift, but the first time he missed and almost lost his grip on the seat belt but managed to grab the brake pedal in time, and that was good, yes, definitely, but it wasn't enough because the cold, the goddamned arctic *cold* turned the pedal to fire against his skin, so he took a deep breath, feeling his throat turn to iron, pressed his chest against the running board, and made a second, frenzied grab for the gearshift, and this time he nailed it, got a solid grip around the thing, and began pulling himself up and forward, his legs kicking out and back as if he were swimming, trying to balance his torso evenly between the seat belt and the gearshift because he wasn't sure how much of his weight either one of them could handle and that's all he'd need, for one of them to snap off or tear away, he'd be royally screwed then, no way could he get another grip in time, and for a moment he pictured himself freefalling away from the car, screaming as he watched the bottom of the car rise higher and higher as he plunged down into whatever in the hell waited below—if *anything* waited below—and forced himself not to think about it, just kept concentrating on keeping his weight balanced and his grips firm as he put his shoulders into it, rolling them slowly forward, then back, forward, then back, and soon he felt his hand slide *up* the seat belt, felt his elbow touch the edge of the running board, and as soon as the first elbow was inside and locked in place the rest was easy. He twisted sideways and lay his left shoulder on the floor, shifting the majority of his weight onto the gearshift and praying that it would hold, and it did, and soon there was his knee coming over the edge of the running board, his hand sliding a little farther up the seat belt, and with a last, painful effort, he got the rest of himself back into the car and onto the seat, still clutching the seatbelt that he at once pulled across his chest and locked into place, throwing his head back against the headrest and pulling in strained breaths, trying to stop his heart from triphammering right out of his chest.

It took a small eternity for him to stop shuddering, and by the time he was able to move again, he realized that the door was still standing open. He pulled his head forward and reached out for the door, gripping the inside handle, and he started to close it, he knew this without looking because he could feel the force he was putting into it, but then he made a big mistake: he looked out.

And what he saw was nothing. *Nothingness*. Only a wide, deep, endless blackness with no varying degrees like a normal night possessed, some shadows darker than others, giving it discernable boundaries, recognizable limits, something he could distinguish as being part of the world he knew. No, not this. *This* was the end of everything, where it all came crashing down, where it all scrambled into an instantaneous decay pattern and reduced everything to a harmless spray of subparticles that were scattered about only to be absorbed by whatever had existed here before the universe had been born.

He *knew* all of this with that odd certainty that every human being experiences at least once in their lifetime, an unbreakable conviction that they and they alone have just realized something that they can never hope to express to others with a tool so pitiful as mere language.

He looked out the windshield and saw the snow-covered highway before him; he looked to his right and saw the abandoned SUV still idling in the emergency lane, its wipers still singing their song of *thunka-thunka-thunk!*, the exhaust from its pipes swirling into the winter air, creating small misty whirlpools that seemed to be trying to resolve themselves into definite shapes.

Matt closed the door, lowered his head, and silently uttered a prayer for safety and deliverance to a God he'd never really believed in nor disbelieved was there to hear such pathetic requests, but pray he did.

And then he did something that he suspected wasn't a very good idea, but he had to know, had to be sure. He pressed the button on the door handle and began lowering his window.

It took only a few seconds for the window to drop halfway down, and that was all Matt needed: through the lower half of the window he could see the highway on which his car was for the moment stopped; but above, in that space where the rest of the window had been, he saw only the blackness of space illimitable, pressing toward him, a few tendrils whispering against the door, curling upward like the darkest smoke, and beginning to spill into the car.

He raised the window a few moments before the first tendril of nothingness could make it inside. From the floor, the voice from the cell phone was still repeating, "…never to stop. The best way to get there is never to stop. The best way…"

The headlights he'd seen earlier were no closer now than they had been before. Matt wondered if the vehicle was moving at all, or if it was only occupying the same space, over and endlessly, while the road below it moved, giving the driver the sense that he was in control.

He looked at the SUV once more as he put the car in gear, and then remembered—

—jesusgodhowcouldyouforget?—

—how he and Lauren had looked at an SUV just like this one during the third month of her pregnancy, how she'd convinced him that, with a new baby and all the tons of new-baby-caring-for paraphernalia they'd have to haul around every day, they were going to need a vehicle like this. There was going to be a *lot* of stuff, you know. And if the weather was bad and they needed to take the baby to the hospital, didn't they want a vehicle they knew they could depend on to get them there? And think of all the *groceries* they'd have to buy every week. Don't you think this would be just so *perfect?*

He drove away, mind and body numbed beyond anything he'd ever experienced. He kept driving until he saw the **EXIT** sign up ahead, then the exit, and he took it, and no sooner had he gotten back onto the road than a **Merge Right** sign appeared, then another abandoned vehicle in the emergency lane, taillights flickering, a Ford Escort this time, just like the one he'd been driving when he and Lauren had first been dating, and he kept driving, kept following the directions every time a **Merge Right** sign told him to do so, kept passing other vehicles abandoned in the emergency lane; **Merge Right**—the Honda he'd driven during his last year of high school; **Merge Right**—the Toyota that Lauren's parents had given her for her college graduation; **Merge Right**—and the rusty, damn-near dilapidated Chevy station wagon he and Lauren had once taken for a test drive from a used car lot, just for shits and giggles, and in which, on a crisp autumn afternoon, he had proposed to her, and she had said yes.

Merge Right. Decay patterns. Particles scattering.

He stared at the snow that came spraying forward from the darkness to throw itself on his windshield only to be scattered by the wipers, and he thought about decay, and loneliness, and grief, and responsibility.

He slowed the car and looked into the rear-view mirror, watching as the exhaust danced into the night, combined with the swirling snow, and danced a ballet of form, becoming the faces of every person he'd ever hurt, ever disappointed, ever let down, lied to, betrayed, mocked, ignored, or—worst of all—forgotten about. They danced around his car with a cold grace, and continued to dance around as he inched forward, never touching any of them, until, at last, he came to a stop and put the car in **Park**.

"I knew after about fifteen minutes," he said to Lauren, looking at her, there, scattered particles trapped in her jar. "I knew what you were going to do, and I did nothing to stop it. I couldn't move, baby. I was too scared. I couldn't imagine how I was going to handle it, having to deal with the baby's death *and* taking care of you, trying to nurse you back to health, spending the rest of my life worrying that you were going to try it again the minute you were out of my sight, never knowing if you'd ever get over it, the two of us always looking at each other and seeing only the third person in our family who wasn't there." He turned to face her. "Do you understand?"

I know, honey. I just needed to hear you say it.

"And I still feel like you abandoned me, and sometimes…ohgod, baby…sometimes I really, *really* hate you for it."

Now it's part of the world, that thought of yours. You have spoken it aloud. You have given it form.

"So what am I supposed to do now, baby? How am I supposed to keep my promise to you?"

Leave me here.

"I can't…can't do that."

"It's okay, Daddy," said the voice from the cell phone, once again that of the child, of Cynthia, his little girl who almost was.

Matt leaned over and unstrapped the urn, bringing it to his chest and cradling it with all the tenderness he could muster.

Just open the door and step outside, honey. The ground will be there this time.

"I don't want to leave you."

You're not. You're just scattering some useless particles, that's all.

Matt unbuckled his seat belt and opened the door. True to Lauren's word, the ground was still there. He climbed out into the icy night and stood upon the swirling snow that wound around his ankles, holding him in place as the others, the figures of mist and snow and exhaust, continued dancing around his car. He spotted the faces of his own parents among them and whispered, "You two would've made *terrific* grandparents."

He removed the lid from the urn and tossed it into the car, and then, slowly, with great deliberation, raised the urn over his head, turned into the wind, and emptied its contents into the winter night. He did not notice that a good portion of the ashes had fallen into a small pile near his feet.

He climbed back into the car, replaced the urn's lid, strapped it into place once again, and began driving away, closing the door only after the car started moving; he wanted one last breath of the night wind; perhaps some of her still lingered near and he could breathe her in, have her with him forever and always, a part of him, absorbed into his tissue, never to be taken away again.

"Matt?" came her voice from the cell phone.

He leaned over and picked it up. "Yeah, baby?"

"Where are you going?"

"Home, I guess. If I can find the way."

"Honey?"

"Yeah…?"

"You have to forgive yourself first."

"For not saving you?"

"For all of it. For everything. You'll never find your way home if you don't."

He stared out into the snow and darkness, and thought of all the sins, mortal and those of omission, that he had ever committed, all the people he'd hurt, turned away from, alienated, or ridiculed. He realized, with a smile, that he'd been a pretty selfish man for most of his life, and not a particularly *good* man, either. All the goodness, it seemed, he'd been saving for Lauren, and for their child, and what good was it now?

"I don't think that's going to happen anytime soon, baby."

"Then it's going to be a long drive back."

"Tell me about it."

"Remember, Daddy," said Cynthia. "The best way to get home is to keep driving and never to stop. Never to stop. Never…."

And as Matt's car was swallowed by the snow and darkness, a wind came up from the south, softly, with almost no sound, and took hold of the remaining ashes, swirling them around in a final dance before scattering them, one by one, into the night air where they drifted for only a moment before surrendering to the decay pattern and vanishing into nothingness, leaving only the drifting snow, the sighing of the wind, and the figures of the mist dancers; soon they, too, began to break apart and scatter, until, at last, there was no sign any of them had ever been there or that any of it had even happened.

But had someone else been there, had they listened carefully, they might have heard the faint, distant echo of a child's voice, urging Daddy never to stop, never to stop, never to stop.